BLOOD
OVER
BADGE

By Wayne Farquhar

Dotty,
Cuddle up and Enjoy!

Wayne Farquhar

1

Blood Over Badge
By Wayne Farquhar
Copyright © 2008 by Wayne Farquhar
ISBN #: 978-0-557-01417-0

Book Cover Design by: Mandi Metzgar, www.mandimetzgar.com
Interior Layout by: Bear Press Editorial Services, Baltimore
Published by: Lu Lu, Inc., www.lulu.com

Advance praise for Blood Over Badge...

"Wayne Farquhar is a cop's cop, and he writes like it. He's been on the front lines of the war on crime for decades. He's got a great ear for dialogue and a cop's attention to detail. When it comes to crime fiction, there is no one better."

-Greg Kihn, author of
The Horror Show *and* Mojo Hand

"A terrific read. Wayne Farquhar knows of what he writes. 'Blood over Badge' may be fiction at its best. But it's Wayne's real life experiences that make this novel come to life."

-Brian Banmiller, National Business
Correspondent, CBS News Radio

"Farquhar writes with the authority of one who's seen the system up close. From tragic threads involving criminals, victims, cops and media he weaves a suspenseful tale that will carry you to the last page, and leave you wanting a sequel."

-Peter Heyrman, author of Hobson's
Choice *and* The North Baltimore Stories

DEDICATION

This book is dedicated to my son, Christian. I was able to finish this book because I had the loving support of my wife, Cari, the inspiration of my good friend, Greg Kihn and the wonderful talent and expertise of my editor, Peter Heyrman.

ONE

Kyle Sanders fidgeted and his ankle shackles clinked. One of the jurors peered at him with a look of disgust. He tried to stay still just like his lawyer, Douglas Taylor, had told him, but it was hard while chained up like a dog.

The hotshot lawyer had taken the case only because the court told him to... something owed to someone somewhere. In 18 months of meetings and court dates Taylor never once let his eyes meet Kyle's. To Kyle, that meant the guy was a coward and crooked. He probably had a Mercedes, two homes and belonged to the Country Club. Privileged people like Taylor viewed Kyle as a monster.

Lawyer and client had rehearsed everything necessary for the trial. Taylor told him how to act remorseful and said Kyle should never speak.

Kyle had started telling Taylor everything about the murder, but when he began to talk about the tingling and the physical rush of killing another person, Taylor had stopped him.

"No thanks," Taylor said. "I only need to know the facts. Save the rest for your cellmate or a priest."

Kyle understood immediately. Why bother with the truth? The truth wouldn't help Taylor win an acquittal of an obviously guilty monster, so he wasn't interested.

Taylor swallowed hard. "We'll call it a victory if I can keep you alive. Where there's life, there's hope."

Kyle nearly laughed out loud. Like *his* fate, the fate of a murderer meant anything to Taylor. Life in Angola was hardly better than death, but he would take it. Taylor was right about one thing: Maybe, in ten or fifteen years, he'd get a parole hearing. Kyle considered breaking out a more likely scenario.

Taylor was accustomed to twisting the facts to fit the circumstances. He once said, "Nothing is a lie. The Constitution requires me to defend my client as well as possible." Kyle learned "as well as possible" meant getting creative. Kyle knew Taylor would have to be creative today. This was closing arguments-the last chance to sell the jury on the idea that Kyle was something less than a total monster.

Alicia Clarke was one of the best deputy district attorneys in the Parrish. She could sway any male juror just by looking at him. Even the disgusted expression she gave Kyle was enough to make him masturbate. Her big breasts and pouty lips would have done it, but the way she pulled her hair back and wore reading glasses suggested sex. She was the bitch who got what she wanted. What would she know or care about a guy like Kyle? How could she begin to imagine being raised by a crack whore who made a point of telling you that you were nothing but the wrong end of a busted condom, and the only thing you were worth was a few extra bucks on the welfare check? That money never paid for Kyle's welfare. Nor his half-brother's.

Alicia Clarke couldn't and wouldn't understand, and that pissed Kyle off, making her even hotter. Now she started her closing argument.

As Alicia mixed damning logic with subliminal sex, Kyle could see Taylor wanted to screw her too. No one could miss that. But the defense lawyer also gave her a grudging professional respect. "She'll be good," he'd said, and he'd been right. She was.

Once Alicia finished her stage it was the defense's turn. She would get another chance afterwards-the last word. The People always did because they had the burden of proof. Taylor only had to create reasonable doubt.

Sometimes, Kyle could smell the sour acidic odor

on Taylor's breath when the lawyer leaned in close to his face, whispering something. He looked like he was struggling between doing his sworn duty and vomiting on his suit.

"I'm up," he breathed in Kyle's ear. "Our shot." As Taylor stood up, Kyle hoped none of the jurors smelled his lawyer's sour exhalations.

Taylor's chair creaked as he pushed it back from the table. Now it was time to argue for freedom, or at least something less than death.

A spark lit Kyle's dark eyes. He saw Taylor put his hand on the table to help himself up. The lawyer looked fatigued. Kyle knew all eyes were on him. *Don't show nervousness.* Hot sensations raced through his intestines as he fought the urge to defecate. The hum of air-conditioning and cool florescent light were only starting to dent Louisiana's hot summer morning. Even through sealed windows they could hear crickets. Most of the jurors had driven here on muddy roads.

"Ladies and Gentlemen of the Jury, thank you for all your patience and attention through the course of this trial. Each of you has given grueling days, and no doubt, sleepless nights to your judicial tasks, and I know I speak for the whole court when I express my gratitude to each and every one of you."

Taylor's booming voice reverberated through the silence of the courtroom. He tilted his head back and gave a slight smile as he opened his hands and arms to the jurors. He was well trained in the arts of sincerity.

"Now is time for judgment. Now you must weigh the intentions and actions of every witness. The prosecutor argues that Kyle Sanders is a cold-blooded murderer, that Kyle Sanders walked into that store planning to kill the man behind the counter, that Kyle Sanders enjoyed shooting and killing his long-time neighbor. I beg to differ."

Kyle liked what Taylor was saying. The lawyer painted a picture of a scared 18-year-old. The truth wasn't that good. Kyle had pulled the trigger and grinned as blood spattered back in his face-- point blank range. The bullet had shattered Mr. Whitman's skull, atomizing blood and brain matter into a fatal mist. He'd tasted that bloody vapor. He'd crowed over Mr. Whitman's lifeless body, and felt an ecstatic rush from the sight of the exploded head.

"Mr. Sanders made mistakes in life. As a young boy, he suffered years of abuse from drunken parents, as well as others who were misguided and desperate. By the time Mr. Sanders turned 16 he had been abandoned by everyone close to him. Robbed of the chance to finish his education, Mr. Sanders was no different than the ones lucky enough to ride the school bus or sit in Sunday school."

Kyle saw Taylor suddenly pause and breathe. *Is he disguising his true emotions—or showing them he feels for me?*

Taylor recovered and began working into his rhythm. The jurors followed, focusing, curious, nodding with each word and move. In the course of a gesture, Kyle saw Taylor glimpse at him. The jurors' eyes followed and fell upon him. Kyle only imagined what they saw: shoulders rounded into a small clump, eyes staring into the hard shine of the wooden table, jagged teeth hidden behind pursed lips.

Taylor walked over and stood next to him. Kyle's skin crawled as he sensed Taylor was going to touch him. But Taylor's fingers hesitated. Instead he strolled around the table. He methodically moved towards the jury. They were hanging on his every word. Their eyes were fixed on his face.

"We cannot forgive Mr. Sanders. After all, a life was lost. We all wish we could change that. But let's focus on why. Let's be fair when deciding Kyle's future.

"The prosecutor wants you to believe that my client drafted a plan, and intentionally shot Mr. Whitman. I believe we have shown you a different Mr. Sanders.

"We have introduced the real Mr. Sanders. The young intoxicated country boy who panicked after he accidentally shot Mr. Whitman. Mr. Sanders went into that store for one reason. He only wanted to steal beer so he could keep drinking that hot summer night. When Mr. Whitman tried to stop him, he panicked and pulled a gun to escape. It was at that tragic moment, the gun accidentally went off and Mr. Whitman was hit. My client was devastated by what he had done. He was a frightened child, he ran away like all kids do when they get into trouble. Certainly, each of you has known children, or have children of your own."

Kyle *was* afraid when it happened. That part was true.

"He made a horrible mistake and he ran like a child. Today, he is before you, wishing he could turn back time, and undo that mistake. Ladies and gentlemen, I ask you to resist compounding one mistake with another. A verdict of murder in the first degree would be a mistake. Please, look at him. Kyle is a young boy who made a terrible error. The law has given you the power to be merciful. Thank you."

The knot in Kyle's gut loosened. Taylor delivered just as he had planned. Polished. Kyle thought: *I couldn't be a total monster. After all, I'm nowhere near as big a liar as that sack of shit.* Still, he couldn't help but admire Taylor's brazen speech.

Taylor sat down and folded his hands on top of the table. Kyle looked at him but Taylor didn't dare share the glance. He was staring forward and appeared lost in thought.

I hope they really believe him, Kyle thought. He returned his gaze to the polished table and saw his gaunt reflection staring back at him.

Kyle felt a nudge on his arm. "Now it's their turn again," Taylor said.

Alicia got up. She was in full stride, performing exactly as Taylor said she would. Her strong, confident voice never had to strain for the correct word. Every movement was purposeful. Alicia was a worthy opponent. To steal a win from her would be an accomplishment.

"Ladies and gentlemen of the jury, I will not waste time in my final argument. However, I do have to address a couple of issues Mr. Taylor brought up." Alicia walked to the display table. The hum of the overhead projector filled the courtroom.

"Deputy, please dim the lights."

The photograph exploded onto the large screen. Kyle saw the picture of his twisted face appear. It showed him smiling, revealing his rotten devilish teeth. He was unshaven with scrappy growth on his chin and sideburns. His eyes looked beady and bloodshot. His frozen black pupils pierced the screen. The white tiled wall in the background was clean and institutional. The flash of the booking photo camera defined its subject in stark relief. Kyle vaguely recalled his arrogant pose. He'd been loaded on crank when the cops finally caught up with him. Now several jurors glanced at the screen, then at him.

"I have only two exhibits to show you," Alicia said. "I realize you have already seen them along with the many others, but please, ladies and gentlemen, be patient."

Alicia spoke so softly that Kyle had to strain to hear her. Then he noticed the jurors leaning forward, listening intently. She was doing it on purpose!

Taylor shook his head. He recognized the trick, and was impressed.

"Please, have one more look at the photograph taken of Mr. Sanders after he was arrested for murdering Mr. Whitman. In searching those eyes, I have great difficulty in finding a troubled little boy." Alicia's eyes flared and her penciled brown eyebrows arched. "I see an evil, twisted man!"

Her suddenly commanding tone startled Kyle. Several of the jurors must have been surprised too. Their wooden seats creaked. Alicia turned and pointed directly at him. He noticed her long slender finger with clear polish on the nail.

"A grown man... who was completely aware of his actions." She paused a moment. "You may see it the way I do, I believe Mr. Sanders appears to be enjoying himself in this picture!" She allowed the suggestion to sink in. Several jurors nodded.

"Let's move on." The second picture exploded onto the screen with even greater impact. Jurors rocked back in their seats. It was the crime scene photograph of Mr. Whitman's crumpled body, lying on the floor behind the cash register counter. His blood and brain matter were spattered everywhere. Much of it pooled thickly on the floor. The empty cash register drawer cast a shadow across the corpse, its currency holders all flipped upward.

Kyle heard quiet sobs from the courtroom. He remembered that Mr. Whitman's family and friends were sitting directly behind him. "Don't ever look at any of them," Taylor had said more than once.

Now Alicia raised her arm to the picture. "Accident! I fail to see the accident Mr. Taylor described. I see a man who was deliberately robbed, then murdered in cold blood!"

Kyle thought Alicia was screaming like a bitch, but her mouth suddenly shut firmly, and he realized she was in complete control. She quieted just long enough for him to hear several quiet sobs. They seemed even more forlorn against the air conditioner's hum.

Alicia's gaze took in the entire jury. Her eyes were wide. She had their complete attention. "Please take your time and reflect on the statements of the witnesses. Look at the evidence that has been presented before you and don't be fooled by red herrings. Stay focused and look at all the facts. Trust your heart and have the strength to make the right decision, thank you." Alicia clicked off the projector. The picture of Mr. Whitman was gone, but it burned in an after-image like that of a flash bulb.

The people and the defense rested. The judge instructed the jury. They were now the pilots of Kyle's future.

Kyle's guards locked him in a six-foot square cell outside the courtroom. In-custody inmates entering and leaving the courtroom walked right past him. He was directly behind the bailiff's desk on the opposite side of the courtroom wall.

Kyle could hear the bailiff's telephone ring and often heard the bailiff's end of the conversation. Every time the phone sounded, Kyle's stomach got tight. *Was this it? The verdict?*

During the first few days of deliberation, the jury called the bailiff for clarification on various details. The bailiff then called Taylor, who would arrive in court a few minutes later. As this went on Kyle noticed jury deliberation was hard on Taylor. He looked depressed. On one occasion, the breath mint Taylor popped into his mouth couldn't mask the scent of alcohol. It was just after lunch and while they were talking, Taylor's head lazily fell to one side. He mumbled something about 'time spent reflecting on the should-haves and should-not-haves.' Kyle didn't completely understand and didn't care to ask.

Finally the ring of the bailiff's phone awakened Kyle. A moment later he heard the bailiff speaking.

"Mr. Taylor, the jury has reached a verdict." The deputy's voice was stern and professional. "The judge would like you to return to court, sir."

Kyle couldn't sit still. Both his knees were jittery with tension. He bounced around the tiny cell on the balls of his feet. Every nerve in his body was twitching. The door from the courtroom opened and the bailiff's body filled the opening. He was holding ankle shackles in one hand and the key to the cell in the other.

"Time to hear about the rest of your life," The bailiff opened the cell door and threw the ankle shackles on the floor.

The courtroom felt different than before. For the first time, Kyle felt the cool air circulating. The ceiling felt taller and the room seemed larger. The judge's bench was empty. Taylor was already seated at the table. His eyes stared vacantly across the courtroom towards Kyle. Kyle figured Taylor had no clue. Murmurs ran through the audience, and Kyle felt the tension. Many in the crowd jotted things down in small notebooks. They broke their attention to stare at him as he shuffled the short distance from the doorway to his seat. Kyle ignored their stares and sat next to Taylor.

"All rise!" the bailiff's voice thundered over the whispers of the audience.

The courtroom fell silent, with only a few creaking chairs and the swooshing sounds of settling clothes. Taylor nudged Kyle. They both stood.

The door behind the bench swung open and the black-robed judge quickly took his seat. Kyle hardly noticed the jury walked into the courtroom single-file from the rear doors. He was thinking that those were the only doors to freedom.

The jurors took their places in the box. None looked towards his table. "If they avoid looking at you that's bad," Taylor had once told him. Kyle figured it didn't matter much to Taylor now; it was over and out of his hands.

"All be seated. This courtroom is now in session," said the bailiff. He sat, as did everyone in the courtroom.

The judge slammed his gavel twice on his bench. "Juror foreman, have you reached a verdict?"

"Yes your Honor, we have."

"May I have the verdict." It wasn't a question. The deputy walked across the floor, took the paper from the foreman and handed it to the judge.

Kyle couldn't stop his legs from shaking. His ankle shackles clanked. The future of his life was now in the hands of this judge.

The judge was expressionless as he silently read the verdict. He passed the verdict to the clerk.

"Madam Clerk, please read the verdict aloud for the courtroom."

The clerk rose, placed reading glasses on her nose and unfolded the paper.

Kyle saw Taylor wring his fingers. His own palms were sweating. His head spun with thoughts and emotions. He could almost hear the faint words floating in the air like the scent of sweet wildflowers. *Did they say not guilty?*

"We, the members of the jury...find the defendant, Kyle Earl Sanders, *guilty* of murder in the first degree!" The courtroom exploded into applause and sighs of relief. The words jolted him back to reality. The tension broke and Kyle knew it was over. He'd lost.

Taylor sat motionless. His vacant expression never changed. He showed no emotion. Kyle questioned whether Taylor even cared.

The judge pounded his gavel and screamed. "Order in this courtroom! I said, order in this courtroom!" Several minutes passed before the audience settled down.

Kyle slowly stared at each juror, stopping to study every face. Most of the men stared back. All the women turned away. Taylor would have killed him if he did such a thing during the trial. *Why care? It's over.*

He slowly turned to Taylor. How could Kyle respect a lawyer who couldn't even look him in the eye? This was the man who had told him they had a chance.

Kyle then stared at Alicia. She replied with a look of disgust. She didn't look away. *Bitch. She wants to laugh at me.*

As the courtroom buzzed. Kyle returned his gaze to the polished tabletop. He disengaged reality and got lost in his thoughts. *If I ever get outta here, which one am I gonna kill first?* He had plenty of time to decide.

* * *

After living 16 years in Angola State Penitentiary, life wasn't much different than being on the outside. As a matter of fact, life was better in some ways. As a lifer, Kyle got respect in the joint. He also got three hot squares, TV and drugs.

Sixteen years had passed by since that day in court. Kyle's appeals had been denied and he was mostly forgotten. The years had brought routine. Aside from receiving the occasional family letter, nothing seemed to change. Outside the prison the world was changing. High tech was abuzz and jobs were plentiful. Few wanted to work in prisons. Guards were tough to come by.

Louisiana had just finished hiring and training a group of new guards and was ready to spread them around the various prisons. Some were good, others clearly were not. Kyle was always the hunter, preying on the weak, especially in prison, but life was about to change. Kyle would soon learn what it was to be hunted.

TWO

When the new eligibility list went up in the briefing room Inspector Casey Ford couldn't believe his eyes. Officers patted him on the back. "Congratulations Casey! Good job buddy!"

Casey knew from experience that the San Francisco Police Department was a political animal. He doubted that he had the juice to get into Homicide. Obviously, he had a godfather somewhere because his dream had come true; he was officially assigned to that elite branch. His plan was finally coming together.

Casey flushed the urinal and zipped his slacks—his third trip to the toilet in an hour. The coffee was going through him, and his hands jittered from too much caffeine. That just made the butterflies in his stomach jumpier. Casey nervously pulled the knot on his tie; he peered into the mirror. His deep blue eyes were studying and evaluating his own presentation. He realized the importance of the first impression. Four years in the Army and ten years on the police department had taught him one principle: Look your best and be your best. The rest will fall into place.

Casey took a deep breath and walked into the Homicide Unit. He approached his new partner, who looked up and identified him before Casey said a word.

"Hi Casey, welcome aboard, buddy. I'm Jack Paige. We'll be working together."

Casey noticed Jack's smooth, almost soothing voice. He didn't expect that from this bear of a man. Casey had only seen Jack on the news, walking around chaotic homicide scenes. Onscreen Jack always looked confident and calm. He directed others, like cops in the movies. Here in real life he seemed bigger than he had on TV.

"Thanks Jack, It's a pleasure to actually meet you.

I'm looking forward to working with you." Casey extended his hand. Jack's hands were like mallets. He wrapped his around Casey's as if he was holding a baseball and his handshake felt like a vice. Thirty-two years on the force hadn't weakened Jack, at least not physically.

"Your desk is right here next to mine," Jack pointed.

"Perfect. Thank you." Casey sat down and discovered his chair was worn. The rollers stuck and the back support bent too far back when he leaned against it. The padding on the arms was torn. It matched perfectly with the World War II surplus desks scattered around the detective floor. Casey looked around, taking in his new surroundings. The walls were stacked with makeshift shelves holding file folders with case numbers written on the sides.

"Those are all homicide cases," Jack said.

"Are they open or closed?"

"Both. We never close a homicide case until it's solved. Remember? There's no statute of limitations on murder."

"Yeah, I remember." Casey realized murderers only escape justice when they hide themselves, their crimes, or they die.

"Some of the older cases have boxes full of cassette tapes. The newer cases have compact discs. They take a helluva' lot less space."

Casey nodded his head without speaking. He thought about the tapes and compact discs and the entombed voices of people experiencing sorrow, shock and anger: the recordings of the many people who found themselves in the interrogation room of the homicide unit. Every person was there for his or her own unique reasons. Some were willing, others were not.

The stale stench of cigarette and cigar smoke lingered in the room. Smoking was not permitted in the building, but Casey knew that in the middle of the night, in the heat of a murder investigation, simple rules don't always mean much. Cops do what they have to do.

"Bottom line, Casey, we get the job done and don't screw up! No chief wants his department on CNN for screwing up a murder case. Especially ours. Got it?"

Casey didn't answer because Jack wasn't looking for an answer.

"Let's get some coffee," Jack said.

"Sure thing," More coffee... Casey wouldn't protest. He'd smelled burnt coffee since he'd arrived. He saw that he would be following Jack. After all, Jack was the senior partner.

They each grabbed a cup and sat back at their desks.

"Casey, I understand you're a damn good cop."

The compliment startled Casey. He hadn't expected Jack to check up on his reputation, but then again, why wouldn't he?

"You know, Jack, I just do my best."

"You've proven yourself in this department. But, it's just like any other specialized unit around here. You gotta prove yourself all over again."

"Thanks, Jack. I know. I've been through it and I expect it. I respect everyone's reputation and experience. The people in homicide have proven themselves many times over. I will too, in time."

"I know you will. I'm just giving you a friendly reminder."

Casey planned to learn, and keep his mouth shut until he got a "who-done-it" solved. He needed to have a perfect understanding of homicide investigations and their boundaries.

* * *

Jack made it a habit to have his new partner over for dinner. He had been through a number of different partners during his career, and he found that this gave them a chance to get to know one another. But most of all, he wanted Sarah to meet them. Sarah was almost always a supportive wife. There had only been one or two instances over the years when she hadn't agreed with a job Jack accepted. Even at those moments he was lucky to have her. Jack had twelve months until he was eligible to retire, but he knew that in that year he would be spending more time with his new partner than with Sarah. That's why it was best she meet Casey. It doesn't take long for the wife of a homicide detective to understand the relationship between partners.

Sarah sprinkled the steaks with salt and pepper while Jack opened the wine.

"So, Jack, is he married?"

"I don't know. He didn't mention a wife. I didn't see a wedding ring either. Come to think of it. Casey doesn't wear any ring whatsoever."

"Hmmm... have you heard anything about him? His lifestyle or anything?"

"What do you mean?" Jack knew exactly what she meant but wanted to put her on the spot.

"Nothing really Jack. I'm, well...I'm just trying to get a mental picture before he gets here."

"Sarah, I really don't even know him. How 'bout we just give him the benefit of the doubt and get to know him first."

Sarah nodded and gave Jack a smile. "I hope he enjoys a good steak and potato. Hopefully he's not one of those young yuppie cops that only eats vegetables and yogurt."

Jack chuckled. She could always turn up the sweet side, even after twenty-seven years of marriage. Three kids and two grandkids hadn't stopped her. He reached around her waist, wrapping her in his arms. Not too tough a task. She was trim as ever and the familiar smell of her hair made him feel warm. He deeply inhaled and drew her in slowly. He closed his eyes and exhaled. A smile welled up from inside of him.

"You're a pistol, but, I love you," Jack whispered in her ear.

"I love you too, sweetheart. Now finish pouring our wine." Sarah said, as she wiggled free.

* * *

Casey loved the little San Francisco neighborhood. Jack must have bought the house back in the old days when cops could afford to live in the city. The lawn was perfectly manicured, and surrounded with mature junipers and black pines twisting into shapes that reminded Casey of the contour of the cityscape. The fog seeped through the cracks of the jagged hills that separated the city from the sea. It found its way into the rich greenery, as well as the concrete, and wood. It looked like a painting. The Tudor home was cozy. The coping, shutters and trim were painstakingly painted, perfectly accenting the design. It had an incredible hue, reminiscent of old San Francisco. The cobblestone walkway gently curved towards the porch. Orange light spilled through the beveled glass of the front wooden doors.

Casey paused a moment before getting out of the car. He absorbed the environment while trying to free his mind of his negative thoughts. He knew Jack's kids had it made, growing up here with this silver spoon in their mouths. Not every kid has it so good. Casey knew that.

Casey caught the aroma of food cooking before he got to the front door. The sound of soft music drifted out. Shadows passed at a distance on the other side of the beveled glass. Casey rang the bell. As soon as Jack opened the door, the aroma and music came to life, wrapping around Casey's senses.

"Hi Casey. Welcome. Come on in buddy." Jack wore a comfortable pair of cotton pants and a button-down casual shirt. Casey had only seen him in a suit. He looked less intimidating in casual clothes.

"Hello Jack. Thanks for having me. My God, it smells wonderful. What a beautiful home."

"Thanks. We're lucky to have it."

Casey saw a thin, pretty blonde woman enter from the kitchen.

"This is Sarah," Jack said.

"Hello Sarah, I'm Casey Ford," Casey extended his hand.

"Hello, Casey. I'm glad to finally meet you. Jack's said so much about you—all good, of course."

Casey noticed her hand was soft and delicate. Her handshake was gentle and her smile sincere. He knew she was definitely not the one who clipped the shrubbery.

"What can I mix up for you?" Jack asked.

"I'm easy; I'll have whatever you're having."

Casey immediately recognized Jack and Sarah had great taste in design. The front room was furnished with as much attention to detail as the exterior. Rich, dark-colored gumwood-trimmed windows and doorways, and every door had beveled glass and lovely crystal handles. The walls were painted rich colors and the hard wood floors were beautifully polished.

Portraits of children hung on the walls. Jack's family was handsome. The only way Casey could determine generation was by the age of the pictures and the style of the clothes.

"You have a handsome family."

"Thank you, Casey," Sarah smiled.

Casey noticed Sarah accepted the compliment well. She'd obviously heard it repeated over the years. Jack just smiled and nodded, his chin rising slightly. Casey recognized the body language of a proud father. Casey's ability to read body language had kept him alive more than once as a child, and again later, as a soldier then cop.

"Jacky Jr. is our oldest. He's twenty-five." Sarah pointed to the portrait farthest left.

"Yes, he looks a lot like his dad."

Jack chuckled.

Casey thought the photo looked like it was taken during Jack Jr.'s college days. He had the same eyes, square chin and strong look of his father.

"He and his wife, Beth, live in San Diego. They have twin boys, one year old. We're always trying to convince them to bring the grandkids up more often." Sarah's voice only partially masked her disappointment.

Jack added: "Her family's down there and they help out quite a bit with the twins." Jack's frown told the rest of the story.

"Oh, I see...I can understand they need help." It was obviously an issue in this perfect family.

"That's Jenna and that's Jarrod." Sarah was pointing.

Casey thought, *Hmmm...All the kid's names start with "J." Why do parents do that?* He didn't ask.

"Jenna is a senior at UC Santa Cruz. She loves the beach." Sarah's warm smile reappeared.

Casey noticed Jack's smile didn't bounce back. Maybe he wasn't so happy about UC Santa Cruz.

"Jarrod is going to graduate high school this month. He's probably looking at junior college or the military." Sarah didn't sound happy about the latter option.

Casey didn't respond.

Jack spoke to fill the void. "He's got a couple of buddies who think they can see the world while in the military. He still wants to play around." Jack frowned and shook his head.

"Honey, ease up on Jarrod. You know he's a good boy." Sarah cradled Jack's arm as she spoke. She turned to Casey. "Jarrod has always been a wanderer, unlike his father. It drives Jack crazy. Actually, they're too much alike!" Sarah was smiling again and gave Jack a little nudge.

"I think the military is great," Casey said. "I joined the military on my eighteenth birthday. It gave me the chance to be my own person. No baggage if you know what I mean?"

Jack and Sarah didn't answer. They just stared at him.

"They really don't care who you are and where you come from. Just sign up today, son! We'll take care of you from here on out! Recruiters smile and treat you great.

Next thing I heard was: 'You belong to the military boy, get up!'" Casey let out a little chuckle. He looked down towards the floor, paused and reflected for a moment. In a softer voice, almost apologetic, he tried to explain: "I'm just saying, it was good for me you know? Growing up in the south, I didn't have a lot of opportunity." He looked up to see Sarah and Jack staring at him. "If it wasn't for the military, I would have never had the chance to join the police department." Casey smiled and looked back at the portrait of Jerrod.

"Let's sit down. Dinner will be ready in a few minutes. Jack, weren't you supposed to get Casey something to drink?" Sarah was already moving back into the kitchen and Jack was heading for the bar. Casey followed Jack into the family room. The bar area overlooked the dinner table that already had three place settings.

"Help me out Casey, whatcha' drinking? I got it all."

"Bourbon and soda would be great Jack."

"Coming up!"

Casey sat at the table across from Jack. Sarah brought out dinner.

"I hope you're a meat-and-potatoes man Casey. It's one of Jack's favorites."

"Absolutely. Most of my dinners come wrapped in plastic or a paper bag. My idea of a home-cooked meal is ordering Chinese from the family-run Chinese restaurant downstairs from my apartment." Casey chuckled. "Being single and all, I don't have real home cooking. Thanks again for tonight." Casey caught himself shying away and looking downwards, breaking eye contact. He was careful to keep his hands off the table, politely in his lap. The room fell silent for an awkward moment.

"It's kind of strange, Jack, I only knew of you from television. I watched you talking on camera. Do you get over being nervous?"

Jack smiled. "Sure, so will you. Just give it some time." Jack seemed amused that Casey had seen him on

TV.

"Casey, please don't compliment him too much." Sarah smiled as she placed the dinner on the table.

Casey was immediately reminded of the aroma that had surrounded him when Jack first opened the front door.

"So, Casey, you mentioned you were originally from the South?" Sarah peeked over the top of her wine glass as she took a sip, awaiting his response.

Jack was serving a piece of meat and glanced up from his plate.

"Actually, I was raised all around the South. We moved between Georgia, Louisiana and Alabama." Casey looked into his plate. His voice trailed off to almost a whisper. Noise from the knives and forks almost drowned his words. "Didn't have much really...growing up." The pause seemed forever. "Guess that's why the Army was good." Reminiscing about the Army brought a sparkle to his words. It was something good in his life. He rarely spoke about life as a younger man. "I was in basic training at Fort Benning, Georgia, sweating like a dog and learning to be a grunt." He noticed Jack and Sarah stopped eating and were smiling at him.

"How did you find yourself in California?" Sarah asked.

Casey saw that Sarah was good at interviewing people. You didn't see it happening with her, she was so sweet. He would have to be careful. He was never one to reveal too much about his life.

"I had what they call one-station training at Fort Benning. I was Infantry, assigned to a line platoon. I was a rifleman. Basically, it was because I was young and stupid. I mean young and strong." Casey chuckled. "I was strong enough to carry the heavy guns. After fourteen weeks, I was assigned to my primary duty station at Fort Ord in Monterey. It was typical Army thinking, they send you as far away from where you came from. It worked out for me though."

Jack wasn't saying much. He watched and

listened.

"Anyhow, I loved the area. Especially here in the city, so I went to night school and never left. The Army gave me a great background and a great recommendation for the police department."

"I have always had a lot of respect for military personnel, Casey." It was the first thing Jack had said in several minutes. "I wasn't in the military, but I understand the sacrifice, commitment and drive it takes to be successful there."

"Thank you, Jack. I appreciate that." Casey raised his cocktail glass and they toasted to the men and women of the Armed Forces.

***

"Wow, Sara, this is absolutely wonderful!" Casey was devouring his dinner and washing it down with his bourbon and soda.

Sarah smiled while sipping her wine. "Thank you Casey. You're a good eater, like Jack. I can see you two will make good partners."

Casey nodded in agreement. He smiled with tight lips because his mouth was full of food.

"So Casey, do you get to see you're family much? Where did you say they were again?"

Casey had left that open and vague, but Sarah wasn't going to let him get away with it.

"Naw, I'm not a big fan of the weather down south and I really don't have family...to speak of. I left when I was 18 for good reason." He didn't volunteer the reason. Casey wasn't used to talking to people that had real interest in him. He found that most people like to talk about themselves and usually he could spin the focus of the conversation from him, back to them. Most of the time they didn't even notice. It made him a good listener, a good detective. "I've focused on my career. I guess that's why I'm still single. Either that or nobody's willing to put up with me." Casey smiled.

"Well if you hang around with Jack too much, I guarantee you'll stay single." Sarah winked at Jack.

"Now why do you have to be like that? Here we are having a nice time. Where's the love around here?" Jack acted offended.

"Speaking of dating...I hope Jack mentioned you were free to bring anyone you wished tonight?"

Casey nodded at Jack. He saw Jack's eyes flare up at Sarah's last comment.

"Yes, of course he did. I'm not dating anyone, but thank you." *Jack didn't mention anything about a date,* Casey thought. *This would be a good time to cover Jack.* Casey recognized that Sarah and Jack had their own intimate way of teasing and joking. They also hid their frustration with one another well. It had been refined over years of sharing lives and raising a family.

Sarah let the relationship issue go. Casey decided it was a good time to change the subject. "So Jack, how will it work? You know, when we pick up a case?" He was anxious to start learning.

"I'll get a call from the detectives at the scene. If it's a solid homicide or looks at all like a suspicious death, we'll send crime scene guys out and we'll roll out too. I'll get the ball rolling from the phone, give you a call, and we'll decide where to meet." Jack fell into a calm demeanor during his explanation. Obviously, he had done this a hundred times before. He was careful and methodical.

"I know it sounds bad, but I can't wait to get a case," Casey said. "Not that I want someone murdered, but I want to work a homicide."

"We'll pick one up soon, buddy, society guarantees it. Just remember, homicide is just like any other assault, except the victim dies." Jack winked at him.

"Yeah, I guess so." Casey smiled politely. *I know much better than you could ever imagine, buddy.*

Dinner was over and it was getting late. They said their goodbyes on the porch. Casey wanted to be fresh for work. Who knew? Maybe they would get a customer tonight.

* * *

Jack and Sarah washed dishes.

"You're not saying much, Jack."

"About what?"

"You know, about Casey, and how the dinner went."

"To be honest, you were too pushy."

"Jack, I was just trying to figure the guy out!" Sarah put down a plate, faced Jack and dried her hands.

"All I said was give him a chance." Jack kept rinsing dishes and didn't return Sarah's look.

"I get a sense about him and I can't put my finger on it, that's all."

"Sarah, I know you are very perceptive. But please give this guy a chance. That's all, okay?" Jack wasn't in the mood to argue. He wanted to dismiss the whole conversation.

"It's not so easy for me Jack. I'm home wondering if you're okay, while you're out chasing murderers. I know you may have to depend on Casey with your life. I have to feel good about him for my own peace of mind."

Jack felt selfish. He knew that he kept himself from thinking about that from his wife's perspective. He stopped rinsing plates and faced her. "I'm sorry babe, you're right."

Sarah breathed a sigh of relief.

"Let's go to bed," Jack took her hand and they went upstairs.

THREE

The swearing-in ceremony for the new correctional officers was more recruiting effort than anything else-- fanfare. Officers marched around in dress uniforms. Hundreds of family members with cameras sat in folding chairs, waiting for a reason to clap.

Justin Pierce took it all in. It was a happy day. Finally, he was getting his badge. Justin looked forward to starting his career as a Louisiana State Correctional Officer. *The best thing about being a prison guard is that you run your own piece of the world. After all, who the hell is gonna listen to complaints from a bunch of convicts?* Justin grinned, showing teeth stained from years of chewing twisted dried tobacco. Every man in his family chewed Cotton Bowl, at least, every generation he could remember. People watched Justin receive his badge. They even applauded.

When Justin arrived at the prison he found it was better than he'd expected. There was a shortage of guards, so he could work all the overtime he wanted, but first he had to attend the orientation for new guards.

Justin was bored and antsy from sitting in the classroom for the 2-week in-house training program. He didn't completely understand what the instructor was saying when he explained prison issues on a statewide scale, but Justin doubted that was important. He paid attention to day-to-day operations, figuring that was all he needed to know.

Justin had never realized that prisons are like little cities, with their own society, stratified between staff and inmates. He learned to separate inmates by color. Blacks stayed in one area, Mexicans in another and Whites had their spot. If an inmate was in a gang, he couldn't stay too close to a member of a rival gang. If he did they'd kill each other. Lifers and death row inmates stayed in a designated area. Homosexuals, child molesters and cops were completely isolated; everyone wanted to kill them.

During training Justin walked the yard, decks and catwalks. He felt uncomfortable around inmates that weren't locked up. In the main yard area, inmates hung out in groups. The blazing Louisiana sun baked their shirtless tattooed bodies. Justin felt the tension in the air as he walked past them. They watched him and the other guards constantly. They watched other inmates even more. Justin quickly learned that inmates were animals in the wild, always prepared to attack or be attacked. Justin found that no matter where an inmate was housed, he would do push-ups and pull-ups constantly. The bigger and stronger an inmate was, the better his odds for survival.

Justin sat in the classroom waiting for the final class to begin. The guard who was teaching was 6'3" and weighed about 275, about the same size as Justin. The guard carried a large box into the room, and heaved it onto the front table. It clanked then Justin heard sounds of metal settling. The guard wiped his rolled-up sleeve across his brow, then grunted his name. Justin didn't catch it, but he really didn't really care.

"Gentlemen," the guard boomed. "The difference between peace and riot is a delicate balance. The venting of frustration must be controlled so it doesn't become explosive. If you don't understand this concept, lives will be lost. That life may be your own."

It sounded scripted but it sill gave Justin a chill. He would never let that happen.

The guard reached into the box and started pulling out crudely made, edged weapons. He handed different ones to the guards seated up front. "Keep passing them back," he said. "There's plenty to go around."

Weapons of different designs, shapes and sizes passed hands. Once everyone had one or two weapons to examine, the guard stopped, and looked at the class. A hush fell over them as the guard said: "Every weapon you see here was manufactured and confiscated in this prison."

Justin looked down at his weapon: a handle with a sharp, crude blade. It could be an effective killer.

Once the guard saw that he had their complete attention, he said: "There's a helluva lot more where those came from. That's just the ones I could carry." He paused. As the new guards handled their various weapons, he added: "There is no greater issue in prison than respect. Plenty of people get killed in prisons for lack of respect."

The guard had Justin's attention.

"My point is this: Inmates have access to anything they want—cigarettes, sex, drugs, and, as ya'll see, deadly weapons. It's amazing so much can be secreted into cement walls. But, just like on the outside, nothing's free."

Justin decided he would try to work on the decks. Less likelihood of getting hurt.

"My class is short," the guard said, "but, I hope, effective. Remember, when you lock a man in a cell twenty-three hours a day, he has a lot of time to think. They all think about the same thing; how to beat the system. This is just a small example of what these guys come up with. Class over."

* * *

Justin's first assignment was the midnight watch on the Double Red Wing Deck. Here every inmate was a lifer. They wore red pants and red tops whenever they were moved. Most were a select group of murderers and serial rapists. Generally, they were cooperative, resigned to the fact that they would never get out.

In his first few days Justin tried to get a feeling for the place—guards and inmates. The cells were somewhat private, no bars, just cement walls and solid metal doors. Justin learned how to pass food and medications to inmates through the small openings in the doors. Guards had little contact with inmates. Each 8' x 15' cell had a single bunk bed attached to one long wall. Each had a freestanding stainless steel sink and toilet. Most cells were cluttered with letters, books, magazines and court documents. The walls were papered with photographs and hand-drawn pornography.

The midnight shift worked well for Justin. It was lights-out for almost his entire shift, and few other guards were on duty. Justin liked going solo, even if it was more work. Justin had always liked working alone.

The prison was never quiet. One night Justin was startled by an inmate's screaming. He noticed that the training officer next to him didn't move a muscle. The man had eased back in his chair, feet parked on his desk, and when the scream came he didn't raise an eyelid.

"What the hell is that?" Justin asked.

"Don't worry about it. Some inmates scream during the night. They get frustrated in the dark. Their eyes got nothing to focus on so their minds concentrate on being caged up. I guess it drives some guys' nuts. You'll get used to it."

"That sucks if they want sleep."

"Yeah, I guess."

Justin realized the training guard didn't give a damn about anything. He made a mental note of it for later.

After several hours Justin tired of sitting. He tapped the training guard's arm. "Hey, I'm bored. I'm gonna make the rounds."

"Whatever...I'll be right here...sleeping."

Justin walked the deck. His sinuses burned from the re-circulated stench air combined with the pungent bite of ammonia that made up the universal aroma in the prison. Justin cut a corner too short and his shoulder rubbed against the wall. Even the walls stunk. The odor rubbed onto his skin and clothes.

Justin stopped here and there to listen. Beds squeaked. Muffled whimpering was suppressed with pillows. Those noises disguised the sounds of men pleasing themselves. Listening made Justin's loins tingle. He got hard.

The crackle of the walkie-talkie startled him. The lead training guard called him back to the post. They were assembling teams to conduct routine cell searches. Justin arrived as the briefing began.

"We'll break up into 3-man teams. Each team will hit a specific cell. We hit them at the same time so nothing gets flushed down the pot, any questions?"

There were none.

The supervisor gave each team leader a cell number and a set of shackles. Justin followed his team leader to the section that housed the lifers.

They stood quietly outside the cell door, waiting for the electronic lock to click open and the lights to turn on. Justin heard the click. The team leader yanked the heavy metal door open.

Kyle Sanders lay on top of his sheets. He wore only prison-issue underwear. Justin could tell from the shocked look on Kyle's face that the inmate had been asleep.

Justin noticed Kyle's skin, pale and fragile. It hadn't seen much sunshine in 16 years. The inmate's cell and body both had the stale day-to-day stench brought by years of poor hygiene. There were no colognes or deodorants on the shelf above Kyle's sink. Justin figured this guy didn't give a damn.

Justin dropped the shackles on the floor of the cell. "Get up and take off those shorts."

Kyle complied. He rubbed his face with his hands, yawned and shook his head as if to rattle his mind awake. He removed his shorts and stood naked in front of Justin. As Justin directed Kyle moved robotically through the search sequence. Justin paid special attention to Kyle's mouth and rectum, the ports of concealed contraband. Kyle's were clear.

"Put the shackles on your ankles."

Kyle complied, never saying a word.

Justin shackled Kyle's wrists and escorted him from the cell. They moved slowly because Kyle had the "lifer walk," a twelve-inch shuffle ingrained from the exact length of chain that connects the shackles.

Justin returned to the cell and searched through Kyle's paperwork, clothes and toiletry items. It was dirty work. In the air vent Justin found a wick. Kyle had stacked a length of toilet paper and twisted it tighter and tighter until it became a worm-like twine. He took his one contraband match and lit the end of the wick. It had a burning cherry like the tip of incense. The air circulation in the vent kept the wick alive, burning slowly.

Justin carried the wick out and showed it to Kyle. He smiled, and held the wick in front of Kyle's face.

Kyle stood, expressionless.

"What's this doin' in your vent, Sanders?"

"Burnin'"

"I know its burnin' asshole! What do you need it for?"

"Smokin'"

Justin found no other contraband. "What do you have to smoke?"

"Sometimes a cigarette, sometimes crank."

"You're getting rolled up for this, Sanders. It'll cost you thirty days in the hole."

Kyle's expression didn't change as he said: "Oh yeah, one other reason. I keep it there in case I need to light some asshole on fire." Then he smiled.

* * *

After a month of watching and talking to the same inmates, night after night, Justin began to learn the things that made them tick. He saw a side of inmates that most never see. He learned their strengths and probed for their weaknesses. Justin wasn't naïve. He knew they had to pay for their sins. He was going to make sure of it.

* * *

The cell door opened, and painful bright light streaked in. Kyle had to squint. The light felt like shards

35

of glass in his eyes. He hadn't walked more than five steps in a straight line for thirty days. Five steps covered the distance of the eight-foot square cell. He didn't care. Thirty days in the hole was nothing. It built character. A good portion of his sixteen years had been spent in the hole. Kyle had learned the new guard's name: Pierce. He decided he wasn't going to let Pierce mess up his world. As soon as he got back to the deck and his regular cell, he would turn the tables on the guy, and gain some respect. It would cost him another trip to the hole, but it was worth the price.

Kyle shuffled along the deck to his cell. He walked slowly and looked around. There was no need to be in a hurry, especially with twelve-inch steps. He smiled; it felt good to be home.

"Hey Kyle, welcome home," The voice came from behind a cell door next to Kyle's. A couple of inmates cackled as they peered through the holes in their doors.

"Good to be home, Lester!" said Kyle. He chuckled, acting unaffected by thirty days in the hole. "We'll get caught up soon as I get situated." Kyle swayed his shoulders back, and held his chin high as he shuffled. Those who caught a glimpse saw he hadn't been broken.

"Lookin' good, Sanders!" The voices carried a tone of respect.

Kyle's feet were still cold from standing naked on the cement floor. The guard slammed the cell door shut behind him. He looked around his cell. A hurricane had blown through it. Everything was still in the same ransacked condition it had been in when he'd left a month ago. Kyle dressed himself and put on a pair of white socks. He slipped his feet into orange rubber shower thongs. They pushed the socks up between his big toe and second toe. He folded his extra clothes, and stacked them in the corner. He replaced the thin plastic foam-wrapped mattress onto the gray metal bunk frame attached to the wall. He pulled a thin white sheet over the pad and threw his blanket and pillow on top. Then he started on the strewn papers. He separated his personal letters from the other stuff, and began the putting pictures and drawings back onto the walls.

He put the letters back into chronological order, newest on top. Many were from other inmates in other institutions. Most were from women, but some were from men. The content was similar to all prison mail: polite salutation as opener-- *My soul mate Kyle. I hope this letter finds you in good health*-- followed by the inevitable update-- *My attorney has assured me we are moving forward with my appeal. Cocoa sends her love too. She will be leaving us sometime in December, the parole board agreed to let her out this time around*—then on to longings, and sexual fantasy-- *what I'll do to you when I finally see you in the flesh.* Prison mail is fantasy sprinkled lightly with truth and reality.

Kyle had few letters from family. Now and then they would write and give him an update, and maybe put money on his books. He needed money to buy things in the joint.

In the following days Kyle got caught up on what had been going on in world, both inside and outside. He spent his hour of exercise time talking to guys from other areas of the prison.

He got caught up with the happenings on his own deck by way of kites. Kyle was an expert at folding the small scraps of paper with miniature writing on them and using strings to pass them under cell doors. He could communicate privately with anyone with a kite. That way, he didn't have to talk aloud for all the guards to hear.

Television was Kyle's window to life outside. He could read letters and connect them to what he saw on television, in an attempt to figure what people were talking about and seeing in everyday life. He saw what freedom was like; he just never experienced it.

"So Kyle, how you been, man?" Lester had a strong southern accent. He'd spent most of his life in Mississippi, until he got arrested for killing a man.

"You know, Lester, It ain't easy but it ain't no thing either."

"Man, we been havin' a lot of new blood coming through here lately. Shit, I can't keep up with all the new people. You know, guards, inmates. It's getting' crazy man."

"I got some business with that new guard. You heard anything?" Now, Kyle was talking as low as possible. He knew other inmates could hear their conversation.

"Shit, he's just like the rest you know. He's calming his ass down after they rolled ya'll up that last time. Ain't much going on since then." Lester raised his voice a little knowing the guard down the hall might hear. "You know, these assholes come in here like the new dog and got to piss in our bowl. They got to let us know they on the block. It's all a game!"

"Yeah, like that ain't never happened around here before," said Kyle.

Both men started laughing. So did a couple of other inmates listening in on the chatter.

Kyle drifted off to sleep.

The cell lock clicking open startled Kyle awake. He wasn't used to hearing the door unlock in the middle of the night. The door didn't swing open like usual. He was waiting for the rush of guards to do another surprise search. He froze, his senses on high alert. No guards burst in. Kyle heard his heart pounding. He inhaled, trying to calm himself, and figure out what was going on. The door opened slowly. Light spilled into the cell. Kyle saw the silhouette of a large man wearing a jumpsuit and leather duty belt. The guard slipped in and was immediately on top of Kyle, one hand over his mouth. Kyle could feel the weight of the large man. Suddenly the guard grabbed his penis and scrotum. Kyle struggled, but the guard squeezed his genitals, and pains shot into his stomach.

"You and me got a long time to get along boy." Justin held his face close. Kyle inhaled air that Justin had just exhaled. It was bitter with chewing tobacco and stale coffee.

"Guess you and me gonna' learn to get along, real

good." Justin gave Kyle's genitals a little twist. "Now you just keep your mouth shut and nod your head, got it!"

Kyle sweated from the pain, and the weight on top of him.

"Got it boy!" He said with a tight voice as spit formed on his mouth.

Kyle frantically nodded his head. The fingers on his mouth and genitals relaxed.

"I'm glad we agree boy. Like I said, you and me are gonna' get along real good, and you ain't got shit to say about it. I run your world, asshole."

Kyle nodded his head again.

"Good, I'll see you soon," Justin climbed off Kyle, giving Kyle's penis one last painful tug. The guard grinned.

Kyle remained still, frozen.

Justin slipped out just as quickly as he slipped in.

Kyle lay there, his head spinning, as he tried to comprehend. He still tasted spit and smelled rank breath. The pain was still raw. Kyle had been molested. For the first time in his life, he was the victim. *The rules have changed.*

FOUR

The phone's ring ripped the silence of the dark room. Casey fumbled for the receiver. "Hello," he tried to focus on the numbers of the clock. The red blur sharpened into: "1:45." *Someone might be dead.* Casey's heart began to race. *Is it work, or something personal?*

Jack's voice came, tired but business-like. "Hey Casey, we got a customer. Get up, take a leak, turn on the light and grab your notepad. I'll hang on a minute." Jack knew the things men have to take care of when woken suddenly.

Casey followed Jack's directions, adding a splash of cold water to his face. He grabbed his notepad and sat back down on the bed. He shook his head to clear it. It was chilly, sitting in his underwear. He grabbed the phone. "Hi Jack, what's up?"

"Got a call about ten minutes ago. Uniform guys got a call of a suspicious vehicle at a closed gas station in the Marina District. They got there and found a brand new Mercedes Benz, engine warm, but no keys in the ignition. They snooped around and found some blood on the rear bumper. They opened the trunk and found a young woman, Jane Doe. Her hands and feet were bound, and she had a gunshot wound. Execution-style."

"Holy shit," Casey whispered.

"Casey, we got a bigger issue going on here," Jack sounded more serious.

"Bigger? What's up? What could make this bigger?" Casey was almost afraid to hear the answer.

"The Benz might be registered to the Mayor. Same name but different address. We already got brass all over the place. This is gonna be ugly."

"The Mayor of San Francisco! Our Mayor?" Casey couldn't believe what he was hearing.

"Welcome to homicide. Now let me bring you up to speed. The car is registered to an address in Santa Barbara, not the Mayor's home. We got a captain and a tactical team heading out to check on the Mayor at his house, make sure they're secure."

Casey had already written the date, time of his call-out, and location of the murder. His pen raced as he noted every detail. He scribbled a few of his own thoughts as well. The notebook would eventually contain all the details of the investigation in chronological order. It would become evidence, and be dissected by attorneys and judges. All of this had been drilled into Casey, but right now he was just writing.

"The body is still there and the scene is buttoned up," Jack said. "We can meet there."

Casey figured Jack already called the on-scene commander to make sure a large perimeter had been cordoned off securing the crime scene. That should keep the brass and media at bay.

"I'll hop in the shower and suit up. It'll take me about an hour to get there," Casey said.

"Okay, I'll see you there. I'm about the same time out as you." Jack hung up without saying goodbye. This was the Jack that Casey had seen on television.

Water streamed across Casey's back and neck. He wondered about the woman in the trunk. Just hours ago he'd been getting ready for bed. Maybe about that time the victim had been enjoying the evening. Then, something bad happened-- sheer terror. A moment came when she knew she was going to die. She'd woken up and gone through the day, never imagining that she would be murdered. Somewhere out in the city people slept, not knowing that the girl they knew and loved was dead. Their lives would be changed forever. Casey felt odd knowing this before they did. Here, he had this awareness, yet he didn't know her name.

As Casey pulled his suit on a million thoughts ran through his mind. Where is the murderer right now? What's he doing? What's he thinking? What's his plan?

Where's he going? Why? Casey felt nervous at the thought of having to answer all those questions. He used the toilet again.

The chatter on the police radio gave Casey a good idea of what was going on at the scene. He heard references being made to a staging area and units were switching to backup radio channels to talk more privately. The media listened to police scanners, and often beat the police to crime scenes. If the media had known there was a body in the trunk of a car that might be owned by the Mayor, they would have beat the marked units to this scene.

The flashing police lights could be seen ten blocks away. Casey slowed as he approached, and took in the sight. He tried to focus on everything-- landmarks, geography, businesses-- wondering which one might hold a clue or a witness. He reached the outer perimeter. A uniformed patrol officer sat in her car, amber flashers on. Yellow crime scene tape stretched from a tree on one side of the street, to the roof of her car. It wrapped around the radio antenna, then continued to the other side of the street where it was tied to a newspaper stand. This would later be referred to in a police report as the "western outer perimeter."

Casey killed his headlights as he approached. His parking lights were on. Cops learn to do this from day one. Never blind other officers at a scene by driving in with your headlights on. The officer calmly climbed out of her car and raised the tape high enough so the unmarked detective car could drive under. Casey stopped the car midway beneath the tape. He had his badge clipped to the outer breast pocket of his suit.

"Good evening, detective." The female officer smiled.

"Good evening, officer."

They exchanged a few words of pleasantries. This was customary, giving an air of calm.

"Looks like you might be busy for awhile," she said, glancing towards the scene and raising her eyebrows.

"I think you might be right, officer." Casey tilted his

wrist so headlamps of the officer's patrol car could help him read his watch. "Inspector Casey Ford, badge 12454, Homicide. I got about zero-two-fifty-one hours."

"Thank you, sir. Have a good evening." The officer wrote down Casey's name, badge number and time of entry on a notepad. She would incorporate it onto the log she was keeping for her report and turn it into the homicide unit at the end of her shift.

Casey pulled into the outer perimeter and drove towards the next line of tape, about four blocks ahead.

The officer got back in her car to wait for the next arrivals. Those authorized would pass, but her tape was the last stop for the media. They would use zoom lenses to close the six-block distance to the actual scene.

Casey saw several unmarked police vehicles parked outside the next line of tape. He recognized Jack's car, then saw Jack standing near the tape, writing in his notebook. Casey parked his car and wrote in his notebook: "arrived at scene 0251 hrs."

"Hi, Jack. Been here long?"

"Nah, just pulled up." Jack was drawing a diagram of the street and the gas station. He also drew the position of the victim car.

"I like to write down everything I observe when I first arrive." Jack didn't look up from his notebook as he spoke. "Weather conditions, lighting, number and make of the cars on the street, and where they're parked. You know, just about everything I can think of. Everything I see. You never know what will be critical later in the case. I know the crime scene guys will do this all to scale, but we may need it before they get it done."

Casey followed Jack's lead and did the same thing.

Two crime scene detectives approached from the inner perimeter. Their photographers' vests covered casual clothes. Both carried notepads and flashlights. The field lieutenant broke away from a group of sergeants, and walked over. Casey heard another car approach from behind. He looked back and saw an unmarked car with its headlights off. It was Richards, the homicide lieutenant.

Two night detectives came from nearby. Everyone gathered in a circle.

Jack got things started: "What do we have here, folks?"

Phil Foster, the senior night detective spoke quickly, fidgeting: "We got a dandy one, Jack." His skinny fingers rustled through scraps of paper, and pages of his notebook. Phil looked nervous and jittery, but he wasn't flustered. His suit had always hung off his shoulders. When Jack rolled up to a scene, he always felt relief at the sight of Phil, despite the thinness and jitters. He knew Phil would have matters in hand. "The reporting party is on her way to the third floor. She's about twenty-five. She stopped to get some gas, realized the place was closed, but noticed the victim's car. It looked out of place so she called in on her cell, then drove home. Once they figured out what they had, uniforms picked her up at her place." Phil paused until everyone stopped writing.

"Uniforms got here and found the car, keys gone, engine still warm. They spot blood on the rear bumper and figure they might have a live victim in the trunk. So they pop the trunk and find the not-so-live victim." Phil paused again, waiting for his cue to start. Up to this point, he'd led the investigation. This field briefing was the formal process of passing the case to the homicide detectives. "Looks like the Benz is registered to Mayor Russell. Same name but it's out of Santa Barbara. Maybe his daughter? Maybe his lover? Who knows? Anyhow, we got the troops and a captain heading over there to see what the story is, making sure they're not all dead in the house." Nobody was shocked by that thought. Phil went on: "I got two patrol teams doing the canvas on both sides of the street, two blocks in both directions, door-to-door. The field sergeant will supervise them. Also got communications working on locating those responsible for the station to see if they got video rolling or any late night employees." Phil pointed in different directions as he spoke.

"The victim's in bad shape. Looks early twenties, white girl, dressed like she's been out at the clubs. Hands bound behind her back and legs bound. All with duct tape. Looks like a headshot, her head's blown up. Execution-style. A nasty scene."

"Did anyone find a purse?" Jack asked.

"I can fill you in on that, boss," said Andrew Mills, the lead evidence technician. Andrew knew his way around a homicide. He would have been a great homicide detective except for one drawback: he hated interviewing people.

"Thanks Andrew, what's up?" Jack asked.

Jack smiled at Andrew with a respect earned over many years and cases.

"The interior of the car looks pretty clean. No purse that I could see, but we haven't gotten into it yet. She was probably done outside the car, or maybe even in the trunk itself. We won't know until we get her out." Andrew shined his flashlight beam along the street towards the car. "We got a path cleared if you two are ready for a closer look?"

"Thanks, Andrew," Jack folded his notebook shut, and slipped it into his inside coat pocket. "So we don't know if we got a robbery, rape, domestic thing or what?"

"We probably have another crime scene somewhere other than here," Casey chimed in.

Jack was glad to see Casey was thinking and not overwhelmed by his first call-out.

Jack, Casey and Phil followed Andrew in a straight line towards the car. They were all careful to not step on or kick any pieces of evidence. As Jack took up the rear the four men looked like a conga line with flashlights. They stopped several feet from the car trunk.

Coagulated blood had matted the girl's hair. The bright red color seemed to jump to life when the beam from Casey's flashlight struck her upper torso. The duct tape spun around her wrist in a frantic pattern. *She must have fought,* he thought.

To Casey human bodies looked odd when they were dead—like plastic objects. He was far from the first to notice that a body takes on an incredible stillness once life leaves it.

"We'll have to make sure we get fingernail scrapings from her," said Casey, falling into the homicide detective's role like a natural. "If we're lucky, she might have gotten a piece of the suspect under a nail. I don't see any bullet casings around. Maybe they're in the trunk. Maybe he used a revolver." He was starting to get the feeling all homicide detectives get when they're starved for information, when there are more questions than answers. "Hey Jack, think we can get someone to check out the tire treads and the boot soles of all the firefighters and medics that were out here? Let's just double check to make sure they didn't pick up a bullet casing and carry it away in a tire or shoe."

"I'll get one of my guys on that right away," Andrew flipped open his cell phone and hit a number in the memory.

Jack's phone rang. "Hello, this is Jack." He paused listening. "Okay, boss. Can you have the family meet us at the station? Also, have them bring a current photo if you can. That'll give us a jump on a flyer." Jack flipped the phone shut and exhaled deeply. Casey suddenly recognized the bags under Jack's eyes. Jack seemed to age years in seconds. "That was the captain. Looks like our gal here is Lisa Russell, the Mayor's daughter, visiting from Santa Barbara. College break."

The cool moist night air suddenly seemed as if it were biting Casey's neck. He felt the chill down his spine, and pulled his coat tighter. The group fell silent. They all knew the pressure on solving this one had just cranked way up.

"The first forty-eight hours," Jack had said at dinner the night before. "Those are the most critical. If the case goes cold in the first two days we're often sunk." Not an option on this one.

Now Jack asked Andrew: "What time will the autopsy be?"

"Probably around ten. I'll give you a heads up so you guys can get over in time." Andrew knew Jack attended autopsies whenever essential information might be involved.

"Keep me posted on what you got here. Casey and I are heading over to the station. We'll get the reporting party statement banged out, then see if we can positively identify this as Lisa, or not." Jack knew they still couldn't assume this was Mayor Russell's daughter. First step in a homicide investigation: make sure you know who the victim is. Jack and Casey left the crime scene the same way they'd entered it: slowly. Both made notations of time and information.

"I'll follow you in, Jack." Casey glanced down the street and saw the bright lights of camera setups. *Ignore them,* he thought. *There are more important things to worry about.* This was exactly how he was supposed to think.

FIVE

Casey followed Jack from the police department parking lot into the building. When they entered Casey noticed some uniformed officers near the doorway to the homicide unit. The young officers had a deer-in-the-headlights look, eager to help, but not sure what to do. The officers nodded, and cleared the way for the detectives.

Casey smelled coffee brewing for the long night ahead. Lieutenant Richards was already open for business, with the reporting party (the girl who'd called in about the suspicious car) sitting in an interview room.

"Casey, need a cup?" Jack was already pouring from the pot.

"Sure. Thanks,"

The men entered Richards' office for the first of several briefings. Richards sat in a blue adjustable chair behind a desk pushed back from the door. Jack and Casey took the two '70s-style chairs in front. A map of the United States covered one wall, with an American flag hanging opposite that. Other walls had plaques and a collage of police memorabilia. Framed pictures of Richards's family sat on his desk next to a stack of papers. It was the stuff of a career.

The blinds were rolled closed and the fluorescent light bathed everyone in a pale hue. Several video monitors sat on a shelf beneath the flag. Three computer video recorders were lined in the corner behind Jack's chair. The interview rooms were all wired for video and sound, and Richards could monitor them from here.

"Hey Casey, got a hot one right out of the chute," Richards said, raising his bushy eyebrows and grinning.

"Yes sir. Right into the fire, but I'm good with it."

"Good, I expected that. That's why you're here,"

Richards looked towards Jack. "Okay, Jack, what do we got here?"

Jack took his notebook from his pocket. "Looks like it's the Mayor's daughter, Boss. Casey and I got a closer look after you left. She was bound up with tape and shot in the head, at minimum. We're waiting for an update from Andrew. Is the patrol captain here with the family yet?"

"No, he's on his way in with Mayor Russell and his wife," Richards glanced at his wristwatch. "Should be about fifteen minutes. The Chief's coming in too. He's going to notify City Council members as soon as we get positive identification."

"We got the canvas in the neighborhood going. So far, nothing. I also got a call into radio, trying to find the owner or manager for the gas station." Jack checked his notes.

Richards read from a note on his desk. "Radio already called with the information. The owner of the station said he shut down about 11:00 last night, got out of there about 11:45. He didn't see anyone in the lot. No video either. Here's his horsepower." Richards handed the note to Jack.

Jack saw the owner's name and contact information written on the note. He slipped it into his notebook.

"I talked to him on the phone. I'll email you the digital recording." Richards linked the digital recorder on his desk to his computer, clicked the mouse and said, "Done. It's in your email." Every conversation with a potential witness or suspect had to be recorded, though the station owner hadn't been aware of it.

"We'll contact this guy and see if the victim was a regular customer when in town. Maybe she had friends in the area."

"I'll call Andrew," said Casey, "and make sure he gets the phone number of the pay phone at the station. I'll have him process the phone for blood or prints too. We can do a search warrant on the number and find out if our suspect made any calls from the phone before or after."

"Good idea," Jack agreed. "We'll jump on that after the briefing."

Casey made a note of it.

"Boss, we'll start a full work-up on the victim," Jack said. "We'll get a credit history and start tracking her credit cards to see if anyone is using them. Maybe we can get one of the night detectives rolling on that." Jack knew they would have extra resources on this one, so why not start using them.

"I'll get that going," said Richards. "Once we get positive identification, I'll have Andrew take the photo and make a flyer for your canvas."

"Hey Boss, can you get someone started on finding out if there was a bus running out there?" Casey asked. "Also hit up the cab companies and see if they had a pickup? Maybe they can track that down while Jack and I start the interviews."

"Sure. Meanwhile, get the reporting party done and out of here. I don't want that girl to see the Mayor or his wife. Keep them apart. I don't want the general public to know the Russells are involved yet."

"We'll get on it right away." Jack reached behind his chair, grabbed a fresh disc and popped it into the recorder monitoring the interview room. "Let's get going buddy."

Casey followed Jack out of the lieutenant's office. Richards reached for the phone.

Between calls Richards watched the monitor where Jack was interviewing the reporting party. Casey sat, taking notes.

"How did you end up at the gas station?"

"I was...out with friends earlier. I pulled in to get gas and realized it was closed." She paused to blow her nose into the crumpled tissue she was holding.

Richards noticed her hands trembling.

"I'm sorry. It's horrible. Is a woman really dead?"

"Unfortunately, yes." Jack nodded solemnly. "Take your time."

"Something felt wrong. Her car was out of place.

50

Not parked or anything. I drove out and called 911 on my cell phone."

"Did you see anyone around the pay phone?"

"No."

"Did any cabs or buses pull up? Any cars in the area?"

"No. I'm sorry. I'm not much help, am I?"

Jack patted her hand, then gave it a slight reassuring squeeze. "You're doing great. You're brave and very helpful. Thank you for being here."

It was exactly what she needed. She smiled with a new sense of strength. "I drove home and went to bed. A half-hour later, the police called and told me what happened. Now I'm here. It's like a nightmare."

Richards saw she didn't have much to offer and wasn't surprised when Jack wrapped it up. Richards popped the disc from the recorder, wrote her name on it, and added the date and time. He met Jack and Casey outside the interview room and handed them the disc.

"The Chief is talking with the Mayor and his wife. We got the photo of Lisa. I had one of the boys scan it so they could both text it and run a hard copy out to Andrew for confirmation. They also described the clothes she was wearing when she left the house. It looks like it's going to be her, but I want Andrew to see the photo to confirm."

"You got the photo with you?" Jack said.

Richards fished the small photo from his shirt pocket and handed it to Jack.

Jack looked at the photo of the beautiful young woman. Smiling, she was all life and future. He thought of all the pictures of his own children. Moments preserved forever, but what did such images mean when the last one was a bloody death in the trunk of the car?

"Yeah Boss," Jack said. "It's her."

Richards took the photo. Lisa Russell: murder victim number 49 this year in the city of San Francisco— and absolutely, the daughter of the Mayor.

All three men were silent for a moment.

Then Jack said: "How they taking it?"

51

"The Mayor is doing pretty well. The wife's pretty torn up as you can imagine. I think you guys will get a decent interview out of him."

Richards knew the fallout would start with the morning news. "I'll run interference so you guys can concentrate on the case. Freshen up your coffee. It's gonna be a long one. I'll let the chief know about the ID so he can make the notification." Richards knew protocol. "Let's give them time to gather themselves before you do the interview."

He was gone before Jack or Casey spoke.

* * *

Fifteen minutes later Richards watched the monitor. The Mayor and his wife sat in the interview room. There wasn't the slightest hint of the political powerhouse couple who had won the last election, merely, two crushed parents trying to survive a nightmare.

Jack suggested that they make an exception and interview these two together. Richards agreed. A box of tissues sat on the table. Richards saw that both had taken tissues, and both held tight to each other's shaking hands. Their nerves were shredded.

Jack and Casey entered the room. "I'm terribly sorry for your loss Mr. Mayor, Ma'am,"

Jack looked at the floor, his hands folded in front of him. At the sound of his voice the woman broke into tears. She leaned over holding her arms around her abdomen, a mother holding the womb that once held her baby. She wept.

The Mayor put his arm around her and held her close. In a weak and broken voice he rasped: "We're just trying to understand this, Detective. We'll do our best for you."

Jack nodded. "Thank you, sir. I don't know how to make this any easier for you and your family, I'm very sorry."

"Please, call me William and my wife is Susan,"

Susan Russell raised her head and looked at Jack. Her red eyes were swollen with tears. She nodded her head to her husband's words.

"Thank you, sir," Jack avoided the issue of first names by not using names at all. "Can we get either of you something to drink? Coffee or water?"

"Water, please. Susan and I can share."

Casey left the room. He returned a moment later with water.

"This is my partner, Casey Ford."

Russell and his wife nodded.

"Hello sir. I'm very sorry for your loss." Casey put the water on the table, took out his notebook and sat next to Jack.

"First of all sir, I want you to know we will be recording our conversation. There's a hidden microphone and camera in the wall. We use the tape to preserve the interview. I thought you should know that."

In the office Richards nodded. Jack knew that you don't tape-record the Mayor without his knowledge.

"Sir, would you tell us about Lisa, her living conditions?" Jack opened his notebook.

Russell began: "Lisa's twenty-one years old. She's a junior at UC Santa Barbara." His face seemed to squeeze, his eyes closing up to stop tears.

Susan Russell wept and cried out: "My god, she's my baby! Please God, help us!"

Richards saw Jack pause and inhale deeply. Richards was single but Jack had once shared with him his greatest fear: losing a child. He watched as Jack maintained—a professional sitting in a room full of pain.

Pushed over the edge by his wife's outburst, the Mayor's breath escaped, sounding as if he'd just been punched in the stomach. Tears rolled from his eyes. He wrapped his arms around her and buried his face in her hair.

Jack sat, head down, barely holding it together.

Russell composed himself first. "I'm sorry, Detective. It's so difficult."

"I can only imagine, sir. Please don't apologize. I'm sorry we're here tonight."

Richards noticed Jack did not say he understood what they felt. He was sure Jack prayed he would never know what the Russells were feeling.

"She lived in a dorm with some other students."

Richards made a note to have her dorm room secured. They would have to search it.

"Lisa wasn't the perfect student, mostly A's and B's. Although, she was very popular."

Richards noticed the Mayor had started talking about his daughter in past tense. Jack did the same. "Did she speak of boyfriends or dates?"

Russell looked confused, and glanced at his wife. Obviously, Lisa didn't talk to her dad about such things.

Now Lisa's mother finally spoke, her voice little more than a whisper: "No steady boyfriends that she spoke of. Dates yes, but nothing serious. She never brought anyone home to meet us. She'd been home for two days. She was getting caught up with old high school friends." Her voice stopped.

Jack looked back at the Mayor. "Sir, her car?"

"She drove home in her own car. Well, our car. We gave it to her when she first went to school. We wanted her to have a safe dependable car for the long drive back and forth from school."

"We didn't want to see her stranded on the highway," said Susan.

"I understand. How about her activities while she's been home?"

"Lisa's been staying in her old room. She likes sleeping in her old bed. She went out tonight, but I didn't ask where."

Susan Russell spoke of her daughter in the present tense. Richards scribbled another note: "Secure and search her room at her parent's house too. Check phone calls, voice mails and pagers."

In the Lieutenant's office Jack's voice broke into Richards's thoughts, and he looked back at the monitor.

"Sir, I would like to talk to both of you about some issues of the investigation, logistical things that will help us; especially while your family is making preparations. Also, I'll discuss the first steps we will be taking to catch this person." Jack was establishing secure avenues of contact with the parents. No leaks. He knew they needed to get Lisa's rooms secure, both, here and in Santa Barbara.

"Sure, Detective, what can we do?"

"First, sir, Casey and I would like to have some crime scene investigators examine your home. We're especially interested in Lisa's room, but we would like to examine the entire home. Maybe Lisa wrote a note. Maybe dropped it into a garbage can or something. We would also like to check your answering machine, email and voice mails. Maybe someone left Lisa a message." Jack was making notes in his notebook as he spoke. We'll also need Lisa's cell phone number as soon as possible.

"Her cell number is 805-893-0897." His voice was a whisper. "Anything you need, Detective, anything at all." The Mayor looked at the floor.

"We would also like to do the same with Lisa's place in Santa Barbara. Hopefully, we can get the address from you as soon as possible?" It was a polite request. Jack looked towards the floor too. He knew to mirror people as he spoke to them. People subconsciously react to mirrored demeanors by becoming more forthcoming or cooperative.

"Yes, yes of course. Good idea." The Mayor was doing all the talking now. His wife was lost in thought.

"Sir, it would be a good idea that in the future, Casey and I speak with you or your wife directly," Jack said, laying the ground rules. "Can we exchange phone numbers or pagers? I would prefer it to ensure we have no miscommunication. If you have questions, you can ask us directly. This maintains security and integrity during the investigation. As you can imagine sir, there will be great interest in your family."

Susan looked up, flinching at the thought of the media's interest.

Mayor Russell answered, "All right, we appreciate

that too."

"Sir, Casey and I will see if provisions have been made for your family for tonight. We can talk later, after you take care of your daughter and family needs." Jack and Casey got up and left the interview room.

Moments later, they were back in Lieutenant Richards' office with the door closed. The video of the interview played, but the sound was down, leaving a ghostly image of the Mayor and his wife holding one another.

Richards consulted his notebook. "We have our press officer and the Mayor's press officer working on the press release. We also have the Mayor's security detail standing by. Russell and his wife will be staying with relatives until the crime scene investigators get the house processed. I've got the information on where we can find them.

"I also got our Special Operations to provide security at the funeral. As soon as the family decides the plans for the funeral services, we'll develop the security plan. The chief's office already made notifications to the city manager, council members and the governor's office,"

Richards closed his notebook, leaned forward and looked at Jack directly. "Jack, you guys got to put this case down. And fast. No mistakes and zero exceptions." Lieutenant Richards was a master at coordinating resources and making notifications. He wanted his investigators to focus on solving the case.

Jack looked at Casey and nodded his head. "You're right Boss, we will." Both men got up and left.

At his desk Jack banged out a quick paper for Lisa's cell phone records: all calls and all text messages to and from Lisa's phone for the past three months. Jack had done hundreds of these papers; most of the necessary detail was boilerplate.

Jack's phone rang, and when he picked up he recognized Phil Foster's voice. "We wrapped up the neighborhood canvas. Not much from it, Jack. No new witnesses."

"Thanks, Phil. Can you bring your guys in? I'm working on the search warrant for the cell phone and we need a flyer for a larger canvas."

"Got it, Jack. We're on our way."

They needed the larger canvas to find out where she had been, whom she was with and what they were doing. Jack thought about the basics of any murder investigation. *All victims have three lives: A public life, a private life, and a secret life.* Everyone has secrets. He and Casey would have to discover Lisa's.

SIX

The County Coroner's Office is in a single story building bordered by trees and flowers a short drive from the police station. The brick building has a prominently posted street number, but no sign stating its business. Its windows are tinted, and most of the neighbors have no idea what actually happens within. The building's parking lot is secured by a slatted cyclone fence, keeping all ingoing and outgoing cargo private. There's a call box with a keypad at the lot's entrance, and a closed-circuit television camera monitors everything.

This is "The Morgue."

Casey followed Jack into the coroner's lobby. With its table, black vinyl chairs, magazines and box of tissue, it looked like any medical office. Casey noted that there was even a small counter with a sliding glass window. The glass was obscured. A small bell sat on the counter, along with pamphlets with advice on bereavement.

The window slid open. A young woman smiled. "Hello Jack, I haven't seen you in ages. You picked up the homicide with the Mayor's daughter?"

"Yeah, we sure did." Jack reached into his pocket and handed her his business card—SOP. As she took it, Jack said: "This is Casey Ford, my new partner."

"Glad to meet you Casey, First time here?"

"Yes it is. It's a very nice office...ah... you have here, I mean."

The receptionist smiled at Casey's discomfort. "Do you have a business card?"

"Yes, I sure do," Casey fumbled into his pocket and handed his card to the receptionist. He leaned in towards the window and saw that she put the cards in a folder attached to a logbook—part of the documenting system for visitors' names, dates and times, he figured.

"Thank you, I'll buzz you through."

There was a buzz. Jack pushed open a door to the office area behind the window. Casey followed. They passed through a maze of partitions and cubicles, then through a swinging door into a locker room, then into another hallway. A sticky mat pulled all the debris from the soles of their shoes. They entered the staging area. Casey sat down on one of the two chairs while Jack got what they needed.

"Here, put these on," Jack handed Casey two shoe covers and a smock.

Once they were suited up they entered the laboratory. Casey felt the cold bite of chilled air. Rows of overhead fluorescent bulbs cast white light on everything.

The coolness couldn't mask the rank smells of rotten flesh, human innards and formaldehyde. Those permeated nasal passages and taste buds. Seven stainless steel tables sat on the left. Naked bodies lay flat on their backs on three of them. The bodies were different ages, and each had suffered a different manner of death.

The tables could be tilted towards a sink that ran the length of the wall. Each table had a large overhead gooseneck spring-neck faucet with a hose attached. It reminded Casey of the busboy's faucet in the kitchen of the Chinese restaurant below his apartment. Next to each faucet sat a scale. A portable X-Ray machine was pushed into the corner. Lighted panels lined the wall so X-Rays could be viewed.

Casey saw the large green body bag lying on top of a table. The body inside wasn't cooperating, and the bag had contorted. Corpses do move.

"Is she in that bag?" Casey asked.

"Yeah, that's the one. By the looks of the bag, she must be in rigor mortis," Jack said.

"I don't know if you know this, Jack, but, I've never been to one of these."

"Yeah, I figured it out when you were fumbling with the receptionist. To be honest, Casey, I'd never been to one either until I worked homicide."

"Doc Irwin and Larko are getting started in a few minutes, guys. Come on down."

Casey saw that Andrew, the crime scene technician, was already there. Casey kept staring at the bodies. It was a bizarre, morbid but necessary scene. Andrew's equipment was scattered on a table near the body bag. He was fitting a zoom lens on a 35 mm camera. A smaller digital camera, also with a zoom lens, sat on the table. Andrew was dressed like Jack and Casey with the addition of a pair of latex gloves.

Casey walked to the steel table where he studied a white board on an easel. The left side was a laundry list of internal body parts. Next to each was a space to write the weight, and any other comment describing the part. A small portable cart contained several crude surgical tools. The large worn butcher knife didn't look sterilized, nor did the other instruments. A sharpening steel hung on a hook from the cart. An electric bone saw sat next to the butcher knife. A coroner's assistant could butcher and disassemble any human body with those two basic tools. Casey also noticed a large stitching needle with a roll of twine-like suture string. He shivered at the thought of what he was about to see.

Suddenly, the room came to life. Two men walked in. Casey could immediately tell from their demeanors which was Dr. Irwin, the coroner, and which was his assistant, Larko. There were no introductions. People just started doing their jobs.

Irwin wore a headband with a small light attached, reminding Casey of a miner's helmet. The doctor took out a small tape recorder and tested it.

What would make a doctor want to be a coroner? Casey wondered. *There must be a lot of detective work in medicine. That must be part of it.*

Larko approached wearing a large rubber smock and fishing galoshes. His forehead and hair were wrapped in a tie-dyed bandana. He had three earrings in his left ear and two in his right. He wore a band around his head with a Plexiglas facemask attached. The Plexiglas was flipped up like a welder's visor. The assistant grabbed the wooden-handled butcher knife and the steel, and started sharpening. He looked as if he might be about to filet a fish.

Casey had pictured scalpels, not butcher knives, but now he realized there was no reason to be sterile. Dead people don't get infections.

Larko pulled a pair of metal mesh gloves and two pairs of rubber gloves from under the cart. He put on the metal mesh gloves then pulled the two pairs of rubber gloves over the mesh pair. "I wear this stuff so bone fragments won't cut me when I'm up to my elbows in a body," he told Casey.

"I bet." Casey couldn't think of anything else to say. The squeak of casters grated on Casey's ears. Andrew was pushing a metal rolling stairway towards the table. It was the kind you would find in a high-ceilinged warehouse.

Jack took Casey by the arm. "Stand right here, buddy." Jack walked his new partner to a spot ten feet from the metal table, next to the portable X-Ray machine.

Jack nodded upward. "Vent," he said. The air vent directly above their heads made this the coolest, cleanest-smelling spot in the room. Casey loosened his necktie and the top collar button of his shirt. Jack took his notebook from his jacket pocket and began writing.

"Let's get started, gentlemen." Irwin cued Larko, who undid the wire twist on the body bag. "The Coroner's seal was broken and removed by my assistant," Irwin said into the recorder.

Larko unzipped the full length of the bag exposing the body. Casey could clearly see every awkward twist and bend. Lisa Russell was positioned on her left side, bound in the fetal position. Blood was caked in her hair, on her face and on her clothing. Casey could smell her blood. Her eyelids were partially open and her eyes had a glazed dead fish look. Her mouth was slightly open and her body was frozen in position from the rigor mortis that had set in.

"It looks like she was rolling around in the outdoors," Jack said, nodding at leaves, twigs and dirt stuck in the dried blood in her hair and on her clothes.

A camera flash startled Casey. Andrew stood on the top platform of the rolling stairway taking photos. The doctor climbed the same stairway with his own camera and took a photograph. Both men climbed down. Andrew grabbed a small brown paper bag and held it open for the doctor.

"Thank you, Andrew." The Doctor used a pair of tweezers to remove plant and dirt debris from the body and drop them into the bag.

"No problem, Doc." The process took a moment, and required more bags. Andrew numbered each bag.

"Let's get her out," said the doctor.

Larko unzipped the full length of the bag.

"Grab her feet and calves. Don't touch the tape."

The assistant grabbed her feet.

"Here we go," Irwin pulled the bag out from under Lisa, while Larko held her on the table. Her body was still in the same position as had been in the car trunk. Casey blinked at the flashes as the others photographed every detail.

One shoe was missing. "Andrew, do you remember seeing her other shoe in the car?" Casey asked.

"Not off the top of my head. But we haven't done the car yet. We just did the preliminary search. We'll get into it after we finish up here."

"Where do you think she'd been, Jack?" Casey whispered, not wanting to be picked up on the Doctor's recorder.

"Could have been Golden Gate Park. I don't know. Maybe even outside the city limits." Jack changed the subject. "Notice she's missing her right ring finger nail?"

"Yeah, you're right. Looks like she put up a fight. No stamps on her hand either. You know how some nightclubs put stamps on hands when they go through the door. Her clothes are in pretty good shape but, her pants are buttoned and the zipper is down. The shoe being gone is weird, maybe she lost it after she was dead."

"Think it may have been sexual?" Casey asked.

"Hard to tell if it got that far. We'll be sure to get a SART exam done, just to cover all the bases." SART was the Sexual Assault Response Team. There was a countywide protocol on sexual assaults, making sure survivors had proper support and advocates. The other side of the protocol was a system for collecting physical evidence in sexual assault investigations. The systems were designed so nothing would be overlooked.

"Doctor," Jack said, "we'll need a SART exam, and scan for sexually transmitted disease if you can."

"I figured as much," Irwin said, stepping back from the table. "Let's get her undressed and see what the hell happened here."

Andrew began opening the paper bags he would use to individually package each clothing item.

Larko grabbed the victim's legs. It took all of his strength and body weight to straighten Lisa so she would lay flat on her back. There were grotesque snapping sounds as he broke her rigor mortis. He flipped her onto her side so photographs could be taken of the tape job on her wrists and ankles.

"Would you prefer to remove the tape or shall I?" The Doctor asked Andrew. He knew there might be fingerprints on the sticky side of the tape.

"I'll get that Doc. Thanks," Andrew carefully cut away the tape, putting each piece in a separate bag.

Larko undressed the victim, bagging one item at a time, until she was stripped to her bra and panties. Those go to SART, so they can be examined for semen.

"Do we know if she was sexually active last night?" the doctor asked.

"Not that we're aware of, but we haven't traced her evening yet," Jack said.

Larko left, then returned with a shoebox-sized container. He opened the top of the box and removed two envelopes. He took the panties and bra from the victim and placed each one into an envelope. This was the SART kit. He put it on the foot of the metal examination table. Now Irwin and Andrew got busy, taking more photographs from every angle. "Hold that ruler next to her hand," said Irwin. Larko complied. The Doctor snapped the shot. "Now, take the ruler away." Click, another shot.

This was the hand with nail torn off the finger. They placed a plastic ID tag with date and case number with every photo.

When the first photo session was done, Irwin reached into the SART Kit, retrieved a comb, and went to work on the victim's pubic hair. He placed the combings into an envelope and placed it back into the kit. He took pubic pluckings, scraped material from under her remaining fingernails, then took prints of all her fingers and both thumbs. They would need these as elimination prints when processing Lisa's car.

He used pliers and a scalpel to peel off her nails, dropping each one in a small bag. With three large Q-tips he swabbed inside the victim's mouth, vagina and rectum. All would be analyzed for semen presence. When he opened her up, he could do pregnancy and other tests. Right now he moistened the tips of a handful of Q-tips with saline solution, then dabbed various bloody areas of the victim. Each Q-tip was individually packaged with notation of exact location. Any fluid not belonging to the victim would be entered into a DNA database to find a match.

"Let's get her ready for X-Rays." Larko grabbed a hose that hung above, turned it on the body. With a broom-like brush he scrubbed caked blood from the head, face and upper body. He tilted the table so the bloody runoff drained into the sink that ran the length of the wall. He might've been washing a car.

Jack whispered, "I could never understand how the hell he can do that."

"I thought I had seen it all," Casey breathed. "That guy must have no emotions."

"Yeah, but thank God guys like him exist. Every single thing he does is critical."

"I hear ya', but he's still weird," Casey whispered.

Larko grabbed a couple of cotton towels and dried

the victim. He and Irwin visually examined every inch of her body, looking for cuts, bites—any clues. Larko got a gurney from an adjacent room, and he and the Doctor slid the victim onto it. They wheeled her into the room the gurney had come from, then closed the heavy door behind them.

Casey saw a warning light above the door—X-Rays. fifteen minutes later they wheeled her back in, and returned her to the table. Larko placed a large black rubber block under her neck and shoulder blades. Her shoulders and head fell backwards, and her collarbones were thrust upward. It looked as if they were preparing her for sacrifice.

Irwin snapped the large X-Ray film onto the box on the wall. "Looks like we got a bullet, maybe two."

Casey tried to discern bullet fragments from skull fragments. It wasn't easy.

"There's a good-looking fragment here." Irwin pointed to a lighted area, then snapped more frames of film onto the box. "Everything else looks pretty good. Nothing remarkable." The Doctor talked into his recorder as he flicked off the light.

Larko shaved hair from around the entry wound. He glanced up at Casey. "We need a good photo."

"The first cuts are always the worst," Jack warned Casey.

Larko placed the butcher knife under the victim's collarbone, pushing down on the top, pulling with his other hand, and steering around the top of her breast, stopping midway in her chest. He quickly repeated the motion on the other side of her chest. The third cut started at the meeting point of the first two cuts and extended lengthwise, down her stomach, stopping at the top of her pubic hairline. There was no blood. In a corpse the blood pools at the lowest points. Blood anywhere else would indicate the victim was moved after death.

Larko peeled the side flaps open like wings, exposing the entire rib cage. The wings were bright reds and yellows: muscle tissue and subcutaneous fat. The aroma of human innards filled the room.

"Thanks for getting me under the air vent, Jack."

"No problem."

Larko set down the butcher knife and grabbed the bone saw. The saw whined as he cut from under the victim's armpits to the bottom of her ribcage. He grabbed the underside of her ribs and ripped upwards. A sick crack split the air as he tore out ribcage and laid it next to her body.

Casey began to feel lightheaded. *Pretend it's a science project. It's not real.* Casey noticed a sweet smell.

At that moment Irwin said: "She was doing some drinking." With a syringe he took several blood samples. "We'll check her blood for drugs and alcohol, get her blood type, and analyze her stomach contents. Maybe you guys can figure out where she ate."

"Thanks, Doc," Jack said.

"The toxicology results will take several weeks."

"No problem. Hey, Doc, look for some of the date rape and rage drugs too. Rohypnol, Ecstasy, you know, bar stuff?"

"Good idea, Jack. Maybe your girl here got one dumped in her drink."

Larko grabbed a small waste paper can, lined it with a heavy black plastic bag, and put it at the foot of the table below the butcher's scale. He grabbed a metal cook's ladle and began scooping blood from the chest cavity. He looked like he was serving soup in a chow line. As Larko finished, Irwin stepped in with a scalpel, removed the victim's heart and dropped it onto the butcher's scale. As he read off a number, Larko wrote down the weight. The two followed the same process with her liver, kidneys, lungs and spleen. The organs wound up on a cutting board. Irwin sliced flat strips for examination. If there were any abnormalities, foreign objects or any sign the death might have been natural causes, they would find them. Irwin plopped what was left into the plastic-lined pail.

"Looks like she died as a result of what we're going to find in her skull, Jack. No heart attack, stroke or aneurysm here."

"Why would he check for that? Isn't it obvious?" asked Casey.

"It is, but we have to prove she didn't die by any other means. Nothing natural contributed to her death. Only murder."

"Got it."

"How about the pregnancy thing, Doc?" Jack was politely reminding the doctor to examine her uterus.

Irwin fished through the innards of the victim until he located her uterus. He removed it, sliced it open, and searched for any tissue growth. "I'll be sure to get a urine sample from her bladder but I don't see anything. It can be hard to tell, especially if she was in the very early stages."

Irwin cleaned his hands and grabbed his camera. He focused his attention on the top of the victim's head. He tilted her head sideways to get a better view.

"We got some good tattooing here guys, looks like a near contact wound." Casey knew about this: Tattooing is the black and red speckled burns on the skin when the shot is near point blank. Burning gunpowder spits out of the gun barrel, sticks to the skin, and finishes burning, causing the tattoo.

"Pretty big hole Doctor. Looks like a large caliber gun." Casey was trying to get a closer look. He had to peek around Andrew and the Doctor as they were taking the usual photographs.

Irwin put down his camera and grabbed a three-foot long metal rod, and inserted it into the entrance wound. The display indicated the shot was fired from behind the victim, slightly downward in a rear to front direction: execution-style. More photos.

"Let's take a closer look." Irwin stepped away pulling out the rod.

Larko stepped in with his butcher knife. He straightened the victim's head on the table, then began above her right ear. He sliced her scalp around the rear of her ear and followed the nape of her neck to the bottom of her hairline. He turned the knife and sliced across the back of her hairline to the opposite side of her neck. He turned upward and cut behind, then over the top of her left ear. He stopped at her left temple, exactly opposite of where he began. Her skin was still connected across her forehead.

"This is the worst part. I hate this sound," said Jack.

It was an ugly tearing noise, like something glued being peeled from a melon. Larko worked his fingers between the scalp and skull, and pulled. By the time he was finished, her scalp was inverted and resting on her face. There was damaged skin and her hair was bundled into the inside of the peeled cap. Her shattered skull was completely exposed. Andrew and Irwin clicked away with their cameras.

Casey heard the bone saw whining again. This time, the assistant cut a circle around the top of the victim's skull about the size of a soup bowl saucer.

Casey leaned close to Jack. "That burning bone and hair smell is turning my stomach."

"Hang in there. They're almost done. This is the gunshot."

Larko grabbed what looked like an opener for paint cans. He inserted it into the skull and gave it a twist. A loud tearing sound filled their ears as the cap separated from the tough fibrous membrane between the brain and the skull bone. He lifted the cap enough to get his fingers under it and tear it away from the skull.

"My God, her brain is completely blown up," said Andrew.

The bullet had ripped through her brain, turning a portion of it into gelatinous material. Death was instantaneous.

Once the brain was out, Larko took what appeared to be pliers, and went to work near the brain stem. With a twist of his wrist, he tore out the dime-sized pituitary gland.

"That's the single most influential gland in the

human body," Jack said softly. "Controls all the others. They'll test that too."

Irwin sliced the brain into several sections, recovered one large bullet fragment and another smaller bullet jacket. Andrew placed those into plastic containers to be tested for make and caliber. They might have striations, which can sometime serve as a fingerprint for a particular gun.

Andrew looked at the fragments. "Looks big, maybe, a forty-five caliber or a forty-four magnum."

The Doctor plopped the brain into the plastic-lined can. "Looks like were done here gentlemen. Thanks for your company." He smiled, peeled his gloves off and dropped them into the garbage can.

"Hey Doc, please don't release the report when you're done. We need to keep this one under wraps for a bit. Confidential for police investigation stuff." Jack made the request formal. It was necessary by law. Autopsy reports are public information.

"Sure thing Jack, my office will give the usual response to the media."

Casey was due one more shock. Larko pulled the plastic bag from the can, gave it a spin and tied the top into a knot. He dropped the bag into the chest cavity, mashed it around until it was level, then put the ribcage back. He flipped the skin flaps back, unwound some heavy twine and threaded a large needle. With that he stitched her chest back together. Next, he replaced the skullcap and pulled the scalp back into place. The victim's hair flowed back to life. He sutured the scalp just as he had done with her chest.

He grinned at Casey. "The mortician can hide those sutures above her ears."

"They can?"

"Sure...and her hair will cover the other sutures. A pretty dress with a high neckline will cover the sutures in her chest."

"That's hard to believe."

"But it's true. Her family and friends can view her

in an open casket if they want. They won't see a thing. Promise." He winked.

As they left the building bright sunlight pierced Casey's eyes. Even outdoors the smell of human innards seemed to linger.

"Hey Casey, want to get some breakfast?"

"No Jack, I'm not too hungry right now."

"Casey, this is part of it. It's horrible, sure, but we have to deal with it. People like us, and those guys in that office have to step up. We owe it to the victims and their families."

"I understand. And, I will."

"You already have, buddy. Let's get about five or six hours sleep then meet back at the station. We'll watch Andrew process the car. That's a whole lot easier. We got about twenty-four hours before the media gets wind of Lisa's name. Then all hell breaks loose. I'd like to be fresh when that happens."

"Me too Jack. Get some rest. See you in six hours," Casey was figuring out that this would be the pace of the investigation until they got a handle on the preliminaries: work for two days; sleep for five hours, then back to work.

They climbed into their cars and drove home. Casey's head spun. His first homicide case was well underway.

SEVEN

Casey's alarm clock startled him awake. It took him a moment to realize it was six-thirty in the evening, not morning—time for dinner, not breakfast. He needed to shower, then get back on the case. It would be another all-nighter. The steamy water cleared his head, breathing life back into him. His adrenaline started up again.

Casey got in the door of the homicide unit just as Jack hung up the phone.

"Hey Casey, get any sleep?" Jack looked fresh as ever.

"Yeah, it felt good. Did you rest?"

"Yeah, I did." Jack motioned towards the phone. "That was Andrew; he got some sleep too, but now he's on his way to the warehouse to do the car. I thought we might want to meet him there."

"Sounds good." Casey noticed the door was closed to Lieutenant Richards's office. He nodded toward it. "Did you give him an update?"

"Not yet. I just got in myself. I think he's over at the chief's office bringing them up to speed. Let's not get stuck here." Jack stood up and put on his jacket. "I got consent on the car and the house before we kicked them loose last night. They're completely cooperative, so we won't need warrants."

Casey nodded as they headed for Jack's car.

"Have you ever been to the warehouse?" Jack asked.

"A few times when I was in uniform patrol. Once to take pictures of a car involved in a fatal crash. And, I seized a few cars from dope dealers over the years. Is it still hidden over there on Front Street?"

"Yeah, same hot, dusty place."

The warehouse was a big barn in the middle of the

industrial area. Its oversized swinging doors allowed tow trucks to back in. It was just as hot and stifling as Jack had said. Casey felt like he needed oxygen the moment they got inside.

Smashed, beat-up, dust-covered cars were littered across the vast floor. It reminded Casey of old fenced bone yards in his native South. A couple of well-kept-up cars had "Narcotics Unit" placards on the windshields. Most likely these were waiting for asset forfeiture proceedings.

Casey saw Andrew walking around the victim's car. He had bright lights on tripods and was snapping photographs. He'd set up his equipment on a portable table. The scene was similar to the Coroner's Office but this time the car was the evidence, rather than Lisa's body. It would get the same care and attention, but Casey knew this job would be easier on the nerves.

Jack handed Andrew a key. "This ought to help. I got it from her folks last night."

"Thanks Jack."

The car rested above the ground on four jack stands. Andrew grabbed a mechanic's creeper and slid under the car.

"Don't see too much here, Jack. It doesn't look like it's been off road or anything," He pushed himself around the car examining every tire tread, inch-by-inch with his flashlight. "There's gotta be something here that will tell us where this car has been."

A few moments later Jack asked: "You find anything?"

"Nadda!" Andrew pushed himself up from the creeper and slid it away from the car. "Let's see if we can lift a print." Andrew took a fingerprint kit from his bag and opened the bottle of black graphite powder. He began to dust the car.

Sunlight from the high warehouse windows streaked through the dust in the air. It reminded Casey of clouds floating.

Andrew circled the car, stopping occasionally to lift a print. "We got some good prints here guys. Hopefully our guy touched the car and hopefully he's in the computer."

"That's some high hopes, Andrew," Jack said "You think we could be so lucky?

"Not really."

"I'll be a little more hopeful with the tape off the victim."

"I don't think we'll get much off that," said Andrew. "I didn't see much on it when I was cutting it off."

"Then I won't get my hopes up."

Every time Andrew lifted a print, he made notes on the card, then dropped it into his shirt pocket.

"Done with the prints, let's have a closer look inside." Andrew lay across the door jam examining the foot pedals with a flashlight. "I think we got a little dried blood on the gas and break pedals."

"Our guy drove the car after shoving her in the trunk, huh?" Jack said.

"Yeah, I'll get a swab of it to analyze for origin." Andrew swabbed the blood, then measured the distance from the gas pedal to the lumbar area of the seat. He went on to measure how far it was from the base of the seat to the level of the rearview mirror.

Casey watched, wondering what Andrew was doing.

"Add a couple of inches for forehead and hair and I'll have a height estimate," Andrew mumbled.

Casey nodded. "Interesting. I never would've thought of doing that."

"It's an old trick. It doesn't always prove true, but I've been pretty lucky with it. The crooks are pumped up when they do stuff. Sometimes, they overlook the little things."

Andrew made calculations on his notepad. "I think our guy was 6'2" to 6'5", a pretty tall dude, based on the seat position."

"Lisa was only 5'4". She didn't drive into that gas station," Jack said.

Andrew wrapped sticky tape around a hand-held plastic block, and dabbed the interior of the car. He focused on carpet, seats, and door panels. "This will pick up microscopic items that might be evidence. A fiber or hair strand could break the case wide open." When Andrew finished with the blocks he dropped them into a paper bag. "I always fingerprint the interior parts that a suspect would touch without thinking."

Casey watched Andrew fingerprint the rear view mirror, shift lever, seat belt buckle, door handles, turn signal arm, steering wheel and horn button. He lifted several latent prints. "Don't forget to call the coroner's office, Jack. I'll need those elimination prints from the victim."

Casey took out his cell and called, leaving a message saying they would pick up the prints in the morning.

"Thanks Casey."

"Sure thing."

Andrew took the key from his pocket and slid it into the ignition. A bell dinged because the doors were open. With a quick turn of his wrist, the engine started and the car was running. "There's a full tank of gas, Jack. He wasn't thinking about gas when he pulled in there."

"Maybe there was too much heat driving the car around with a body in the trunk." Casey spoke up so they could hear him over the engine noise.

"What station is the radio set on?" Jack asked.

Andrew hit a button, and they heard an old George Jones tune ending. "Something country-western," Andrew said. "What did the victim listen to?" Andrew turned the car off.

"I don't know. We'll ask her folks. I just got the basics out of them last night. We'll get a good interview in the next day or so, maybe when you guys are doing the house?"

"When do you want the house processed?"

"Yesterday...is that too soon?"

"Nope...I hear ya."

Andrew itemized the contents of the glove box and center console. "The garage door opener and registration are still here."

"A burglar would have taken the opener and used the registration to get the address," Jack observed.

Andrew began work in the trunk, snapping photos, then swabbing blood evidence. He seemed to bury his head inside, and Casey saw only shadows and the flashlight beam moving around.

Andrew's voice came up from inside the trunk, seeming strangely disembodied. "We know these things for sure: there's no purse, no keys, no bullet casing, no fingernail and no shoe."

"So we've got a suspect who listens to country-western music and totes a six-shooter, said Casey. "He sounds like a cowboy."

"I think you're right about the revolver," Jack said. "That explains why there's no bullet casing."

"By the looks of the blood spatter, I think our gal was shot somewhere else, then stuffed in the trunk for transportation," said Andrew.

"She had to be. Who would shoot her in the parking lot of the gas station?" Jack's question was rhetorical. Nobody answered.

"I don't see any high-velocity spatter here. Its big drops and drainage-type patterns," Andrew said.

"Maybe it was a semi-auto and the casing was ejected at the murder scene?" Casey was still thinking about the gun.

"Where the hell did the duct tape come from?" Jack asked. "The guy or guys may have been sexual predators. Why the hell else would someone have duct tape with them?"

"What if she was a target?" Casey said. "Maybe, they wanted to take her off because she was the Mayor's daughter. A kidnapping gone bad? Maybe someone wanted to motivate our Mayor on some public issue. Really get his attention."

"When we get back to the station let's contact the Mayor's security staff and check for hot issues, death threats, all that. Also, let's talk to the guys in the Intelligence Unit—get the latest on what's been going on

75

with extremist groups in the area and on the college campuses. Maybe a link between one here with one down in Santa Barbara. The Intel guys have a good handle on that, and we can't overlook any possibilities... not on this one."

Casey and Jack needed to determine two critical locations: where the suspect came into contact with Lisa, then precisely where she was murdered.

Jack's cell phone rang. "This is Jack." He listened a moment. "Thanks, I appreciate the call." Jack frowned as he flipped the phone closed. "We just can't seem to catch a break. That was the cell company. There's no GPS on Lisa's phone...Nada."

Casey nodded. "Bad."

"Andrew, we'll see you back at the station. We need to get a flyer out to the patrol officers on the streets quick."

"All right guys. I'll call Santa Barbara and get her dorm secured."

"Thanks, Andrew, time's a-wastin'." Jack and Casey got back in the car and headed to Homicide.

"We need to start putting controlled information out, Casey. We need a snitch."

"We'll get a ton of calls once we do the press release, right?"

"Oh yeah, they'll start climbing out of the woodwork. Unfortunately, so will the crackpots and kooks."

EIGHT

"Well I'll be damned," Kyle Sanders whispered as he watched the news anchor report the breaking story out of San Francisco. The daughter of that city's Mayor had been a victim of homicide. Kyle stared as figures walked around the crime scene. Police lights flashed, and yellow tape shook in the night breeze. It was footage from a couple of nights earlier, when the victim's identity hadn't yet been released.

Kyle squinted, trying to get a better look at the faces there on the scene. TV lights played on the reporter, and the police tape, but beyond that illumination was poor. The cameraman had focused on the victim's car rather than the investigators. With its 9-inch screen the cheap prison TV wasn't much help either.

Kyle kept studying the picture as a TV reporter interviewed neighbors. They had little or nothing to say. They hadn't seen anything.

A woman in a bathrobe said: "Normally, it's very quiet here." *Yeah,* Kyle thought. *I've heard it a million times. It's always quiet till somebody like me shows up.*

The reporter stretched it as far as it would go, but information was thin. The Mayor's daughter had been murdered and the police had no suspects in custody. The detectives hadn't said how she was killed. Nor was there any hint of a motive.

They're no closer to solving it than I am to getting out of this dump, Kyle thought. He flipped through the channels hoping to get another report. Maybe he would see a better camera angle, or maybe some enterprising reporter would corner some hapless detective and shake out a comment. He found nothing except the same clip. He turned the television off.

* * *

The media wanted a live interview with Casey or Jack. A story came to life when the investigators talked for the record. Maybe they couldn't say much, but at least it put a real person into the mix. Reporters seemed to love unsolved murders as much as cops hated them. Ongoing mysteries involving famous people kept viewers watching and readers reading. It gave a producer a hook to throw out before the commercial. "New clue in homicide—details right after this break." The Mayor's daughter killed—it was a story that could go on for weeks.

Lieutenant Richards and Jack thought it would be good for Casey to provide a live interview. He was well-spoken, and it would give the reporters a chance to meet the newest member of the homicide team. Most of the homicide detectives knew the reporters well. Over the years they'd built relationships based on a balance between secrecy and scoops. Sometimes it worked, other times it didn't. A good reporter might learn information the police wanted to keep under wraps, "hold back" information. If the reporter promised to honor the "hold back" stuff, they knew they would probably be rewarded with some future scoop, usually early notification on a big arrest. Such arrangements built trust between reporters and homicide detectives—the kind of trust that's very common between the police and the media.

Richards and Jack knew that Casey would have to navigate this minefield, and an on-air interview with all of them would be as good an initiation as any.

Casey wasn't used to being the central conduit for information, but he'd seen it done. Prior to coming to homicide he had been involved in cases that attracted media coverage. To get himself ready Casey met with the Department's Press Information Officer or PIO.

Casey could see that the PIO had this job for a reason. The guy had a nice smile and sincerity oozed from his pores. He was as good a "face" as a police department could want, and he knew the ins and outs of talking in front of cameras.

"The most important tip I can give you is: don't say anything you don't want said."

To Casey this seemed ridiculously obvious. "Sorry, but that sounds like common sense to me," he said.

"It does sound like common sense, but it may play out a little differently in an interview. When you go out there, they all have their questions, and what they want is simple: everything. But there's only so much you can tell them. So the key is: only think about what you're supposed to tell them: the information you want to release. It doesn't matter what they ask you. Just say what you have to say. That's all."

"But if they ask a question, and what I say has nothing to do with what they asked, I'll look like a fool."

"No. They expect it. When they show the clip on the air, the question is never shown. It takes too much time. The viewer sees the TV reporter outside the building, giving the background, then they cut right to a clip of you. In reality, the reporter will tailor his report to whatever you've said in front of the camera, so it will all make sense to the viewer." The PIO saw the revelation on Casey's face.

"So, no matter how ridiculous you may feel, say exactly what you want said, even if it's totally non-responsive to the question," Casey said.

The PIO nodded and smiled. This one picked it up fast.

Once Casey had grasped exactly what he was supposed to do, he consulted with Jack.

"What do you think? Should we release the manner of death? You know the reporters will be starving for that."

"No," Jack said. "Hold that back. The news clips haven't had a shot of the body. Let's keep that for later. There's already a million calls from people who 'know.' We have to weed out the bogus ones. This way we can eliminate all the strangulation and suffocation leads, or at least, make them a lower priority."

"My feeling is this," Casey scooted up in his chair. "We stress that we need the help of the public. This is a terrible case and we absolutely need the help of witnesses to backtrack Lisa's evening. We give them the flyer with her picture and the car and ask if anybody saw her or the vehicle. Hopefully, they'll run the flyer long enough for us to flush out a witness."

"Good idea, let's run with it," Jack said. He liked the fact that this guy was thinking.

* * *

The camera lights blinded Casey. He'd never understood why they needed such bright lights in the daytime. Traci Townsend was closest to the podium. She was the field reporter with the top local TV station. She was absolutely stunning and glamorous, her shimmering blond hair accenting her bronze, tanning-salon skin. Her bleached white teeth and red lips added up to a sexy smile. Though she was petite, her expert plastic surgeon had sculpted just the right exaggerations into her breasts and butt. She might as well have made love to the camera. Traci could charm or turn vicious at will.

To Casey she seemed too shallow for either emotion to be real. Like all reporters, she could twist words in interesting fashion. She liked to call victims by their names. Of course, this did humanize the victim, but in this particular case, it also reminded viewers that the victim was the Mayor's daughter.

"Detective, how was Lisa Russell murdered?"

"I'm sorry. We cannot release that information now, it would jeopardize the investigation. We will release that as soon as we are able." Casey's voice had a firm tone.

"Can you tell us if you have any suspects?" a voice asked from the crowd.

"We have not focused the investigation on any single person or group at this time. We are asking for the public's help. If anyone saw Lisa or had contact with her during the past week, please give us a call."

"Was Lisa sexually assaulted?"

Casey looked at Traci. She smiled, her nose

squinting, and tipped her head sideways as if to say, 'it's my job.' She knew she wouldn't be shown asking the question.

"It's very early in the investigation." Casey wanted to smirk at Traci, but didn't dare. Her lips formed a pout. Was this girl flirting with him?

Casey reached into his folder and took out a copy of the flyer they had put together. He held it up so the cameramen would get a good shot. "Here is a picture of Lisa and her car. Please call us if you believe you saw her in the days before she died." Casey was ready to finish.

"Detective, do you think this killer might strike again? Have you considered this might be some type of crazed serial killer on the loose?" Traci loved to turn up the meter on speculation. It pushed up ratings.

"We have no indication this is a serial case." Casey knew he had better address this or her theory would take on a life of its own. "We have been in contact with neighboring jurisdictions and there are no similar cases. We are in the early stages of this investigation and it is critical we not begin to speculate."

Traci saw she was not getting any more information about the homicide, so she shifted the focus. "How are Mayor Russell and his family handling this tragedy?"

"As you can imagine, this is a difficult time for them. It would be for any of us. It's important we show our support and respect. Mayor Russell and his family express their thanks for your thoughts and prayers."

Jack was impressed by Casey's performance on that last one. "That was smooth," he said to Richards.

Casey ended the conference with a plea. "Please look at the flyer and give us a call if you feel you can help us with any information. I'm sorry I can't answer all your questions, but we need to get back to work. Thank you." The conference was over. The media had their tape just in time to edit and cut for the evening news.

Traci approached Casey while her camera crew folded up their gear. Her stride was sexy and her fragrance was fresh and sweet smelling.

"Detective, can we have lunch? Off the record of course." She raised her perfectly painted eyebrows and her green eyes looked directly at him.

The question caught him off guard and she knew it. Casey didn't have a ready reply. "I-I'm pretty tied up as you can imagine," he said.

She held out her card, and smiled. "Here. This has my personal cell number. Don't wait too long to call, sweetie."

Casey knew few men denied attention from Traci. He also knew that everything he'd heard about her from his colleagues was bad news. Despite that, he took the card.

* * *

Kyle flipped off the television, lay back on his bunk and lit a contraband cigarette. He inhaled deep into his lungs, held it, and then relaxed his chest as the smoke rolled from his mouth. He closed his eyes and thought back to childhood when things had seemed so much less complicated. *How did this happen in my life?* He thought about times when he and his brother ran barefoot in the yard. There'd been other kids in the neighborhood— friends even. Kyle had memories of laughing and playing tag. The coarse green crabgrass would make his feet itch.

The weather in those memories was always hot and humid, but an occasional rain shower would cool things down. Late in the day, at sunset, the fireflies would zip around and the armadillos would make their way out of hiding to start rooting in the crabgrass. He could almost smell the pig cooking on the barbecue. He and his brother could hardly wait to check the catfish lines in the creek next to the house. *Who would have known it would end up this way?* Kyle missed his childhood. *Nobody could have ever known.*

Lost in thought, Kyle finished the last of his cigarette. He didn't hear the lock on his cell door click. Suddenly, the door swung open and there in the doorway stood his favorite guard silhouetted against lighter shadows.

"Say hey, Mr. Sanders. Enjoying that smoke?" Justin Pierce gave a twisted smile.

"Since when does anyone give a shit about a smoke?" Kyle asked.

"Whaddya mean? It's a violation."

"But nobody—"

"Quiet!" Justin snapped. He raised his head, sniffing. "I thought I smelled smoke. I sure did. My job is to enforce the rules." His smile turned evil. "I told you!" He paused to take a deep breath, then spoke in a whisper so he couldn't be overheard. "This is my world, asshole."

Kyle felt spit on his face. He couldn't believe this Okie scum was haunting him. All he wanted was to be left alone. Like sixteen years in the joint wasn't already enough. Now he had to deal with this jack-off for the rest of his life.

"Well sir, I'm real sorry." Kyle bent over and snuffed the cigarette out on the floor. As he rose, he smashed his fist between Pierce's legs. Pierce cried out and his legs buckled but he didn't go down. Kyle thought: *I've got a strong one here.* The thought didn't last long because Kyle felt a smashing blow to his left temple. His vision in his left eye narrowed and he felt pain radiating across his forehead. With Justin's quick response, Kyle lost track of what was happening. He could feel blows all over his body but he went numb. Pierce beat the shit out of him with a small wooden billy club. Long before it was over Kyle had lost consciousness,

When he woke up Kyle was stripped naked on the floor of the hole. He could taste blood on his swollen lips, and as he smelled the odor of urine and feces, he wondered if he was lying in them. He tried to feel his body but when he moved he hurt. His whole body hurt. He had never been beaten this badly. He began to recall Pierce standing over him and beating him. There was the cigarette and the fight. He winced, exhaled deeply and fell fast asleep. That was his only escape.

In Pierce's report Inmate Sanders had attacked him while he was enforcing rule. Pierce fought for his life as Inmate Sanders savagely battered him. Pierce overcame Inmate Sanders' resistance and took him into custody. The Warden reviewed the report and was thankful Pierce had not been severely injured. The guard might even get an award. The Warden liked justice to be served in-house. Inmate Sanders would not be criminally charged.

One week in the hole would be his punishment. That would give the beating additional value. The other cons would see the consequences before Sanders had a chance to heal.

Down in the hole Kyle woke again. Three trays of food sat on the floor next to the door. This was the only indication of how long he had been asleep. His head was pounding and fuzzy. He rolled onto his right side to sit up. A sharp pain in his ribs robbed him of breath. He grunted and pushed himself into a seated position. Once he was seated he inventoried himself. He had soiled himself. His eyes and lips were swollen. Kyle struggled to his feet and steadied himself with the steel washbasin. He turned on a trickle of water and began cleaning himself. The cold water helped clear his head. Based on the food trays, he figured he had been in the hole about twenty-four hours.

The door swung open and Pierce was standing in the doorway with another tray of food. He had that same twisted grin. "Only six more days' asshole, then you're close to me again in our private room. I told you, it's my world, not yours." Pierce dropped the tray on the floor and slammed the door shut. Kyle heard a chuckle as footsteps became faint.

There was no television in the hole. Kyle would miss the news for a week. He bent over the sink, splashed cool water on his face and realized something. *Either I gotta' get out of this prison, or I'm gonna' have to kill that asshole."*

NINE

The media was going crazy. The story broke and, as usual city officials began to panic. Jack made two hundred copies of the flyer showing pictures of Lisa and her Mercedes. He and Casey attended as many patrol briefings as possible and distributed the flyers to the street cops. They needed a snitch.

"Jack!" Lieutenant Richards called from the chair in his office. "Grab your partner, come in here a minute."

Jack and Casey went in and sat down. Richards's eyes were more bloodshot, and the bags underneath of them had grown darker. The pressure from the brass was obvious. Jack knew that Richards was absorbing all of it so he and Casey could concentrate on the case. The Lieutenant had always been good at shielding his detectives from political fallout. Jack had a keen appreciation of this. He'd worked for lousy lieutenants, ones who'd only created more pressure. Richards wasn't one of those. He knew how to stay on top of a case without weighing down his men.

"Where you guys with the case?"

"We got flyers out to patrol," said Jack. "We need to do the house, and another interview with the Russells."

"When you getting it done?"

"As soon as we get outta here. Andrew buttoned up the dorm. It should be secure. We need to get down there too."

"What do you need from me?"

"Same thing as usual, Boss, keep the heat off."

"Not easy on this one, boys."

"We understand. Oh yeah, one more thing that Casey came up with."

"Yeah, what's that?" Richards leaned forward and crossed his hands on his desk.

Jack leaned back, looking towards Casey.

Casey started: "Well boss, I just thought maybe, Lisa wasn't a random victim." Casey sat up in his chair. "What if our crook was looking for her specifically so he could leverage the Mayor? Either a kidnap for ransom, or maybe to sway the Mayor on some political issue-- who knows?" Richards was listening.

Jack chimed in. "I think it may be a good angle. It's definitely something we have to look at. What if we hit up the Intelligence folks to look into it?"

"That would sure complicate things." Richards hated to think of it getting that big, but he had to. "You guys think we should beef up the security on the Mayor for a while?"

"That's your call, Boss. That's why you make the big bucks." Jack put his hands up and leaned back in his chair.

Richards picked up the phone and punched four numbers. "This is Lieutenant Richards. I want another security team on the Mayor and his wife until further notice."

Jack heard a voice on the other end of the phone but couldn't make out what they were saying.

"I don't give a shit about the overtime for Christ's sake! Just do it! We're talking about the fucking Mayor here!"

The other end fell silent.

"And you will personally call me when it's done! Am I clear?" Richards slammed the phone down. "Jesus Christ! These guys want everything done but they don't want to spend the money to do it right!" He pointed towards the phone. "They just bust my balls day in and day out!"

The bags under Richards' eyes were darkening by the minute. Jack took that as a cue to leave. He got up and nodded to Casey.

The two detectives headed for the Intel Unit, always a strange place. The detectives there monitored different groups and organizations. They never wrote police reports because those were discoverable under the Freedom of Information Act. Intel detectives monitored terrorist and extremist groups, outlaw motorcycle gangs, prison gangs and any other radical group that might pose a threat to the public or the police. The well-organized groups that pride themselves on civil disobedience plan their tactics well in advance. Intel detectives track such information. A cop or two on the force might have once belonged to an extremist group or even the Communist Party. Intel detectives might be keeping track of them too.

Jack briefed the Intel Unit on the homicide. Casey explained his theory. The Intel guys bit on Casey's theory. Conspiracy linked with politics—it made perfect sense to them. It was in their blood.

* * *

Jack called the Mayor's security to tell them they were heading to the Mayor's house. Mayor Russell deserved advanced notice and Jack didn't want to surprise the security officers. They were bound to be jumpy.

Jack and Casey climbed into Jack's car to head over to the house.

"Jack, should I call Andrew?"

"No. I think we should minimize the intrusion over there. We can collect evidence ourselves. If there's something we can't handle, we'll call Andrew."

The long cobblestone driveway to the house was crescent-shaped and lined with lanterns up on black poles. Years ago, the city had torn up a number of streets and found old cobblestones under the pavement. The cobblestones were sold at auction to contractors. With the huge demand, most walked away empty-handed, but, as luck would have it, the Mayor happened to get enough for his driveway.

The front yard was well covered with mature birch trees. The beautiful white bark of the trees contrasted with the shade. A slight breeze wafted through. Branches swayed and leaves gently fluttered to the ground. Jack felt a great sense of loneliness. The doors of the three-car garage were closed, as were the shutters on the windows of the house.

Though the house looked empty, Jack knew the Russell's were home. Still, he could sense that this was a house that was not open for visitors. He felt sorrow when he saw the house. It looked dark and sad. He thought about his own children and was thankful he never had to deal with that kind of loss. Jack swallowed hard on the lump in his throat. He began to go through what he would say to these people when he was face-to-face with them.

The front doors were beautiful, arched to a point at least ten feet high. The hardwood was polished and aged. They reminded Jack of a grand entrance into a winery he had once visited. When he pushed the doorbell there came the deep ringing of chimes. A moment later Mayor Russell opened the door. Jack could see the Mayor was expecting them.

"Good morning Mayor Russell. I'm not sure you remember, but I'm Jack Paige and this is Casey Ford. We met the other night at the police station."

"Of course I remember, gentlemen," the Mayor bowed his head. "Please come in," He took a step backward, opened the door wide.

Jack stepped in first; Casey followed. The entryway floor had spectacular tile work in a semicircular design. Each piece was cut by hand and fitted into a mosaic. The color combinations were brilliant. Jack had an appreciation for tiles. He'd seen some of the best in European churches many years earlier, and their beauty had never left his memory.

"Would you gentleman like something to drink? Coffee, tea, anything?" The Mayor motioned towards the kitchen.

"Oh, no thank you, sir. We're fine. Is there someplace we can sit for a few minutes and talk?"

"Of course, right this way."

They followed the Mayor into the kitchen. It reminded Jack of the perfect kitchens in cooking shows on television. Stainless steel appliances sat on marble counter tops. Yet the room suddenly felt cold as Jack heard the slight echo of his own footsteps. They sat at a slightly distressed, stained-wood table. It didn't seem very old.

Jack set his ideas on décor aside, and took out a notebook. Mr. Mayor, we were wondering if you or your family has received any threats?"

The Mayor looked puzzled. "No. Well, not that I can think of. Nothing here at the house." He slowly shook his head as he looked towards the ground. His voice was low and unsteady. "My staff always notifies me if anyone threatens me at the office. But, I haven't had anything like that in a long time."

Jack leaned forward to hear. "Sir, I ask because it's something we have to look at." Jack glanced at Casey and could see his partner nod in agreement.

"Do you gentlemen believe someone might have done this to Lisa in order to hurt me?"

"Again, sir, we look at every angle. We cannot, and will not, leave any stone unturned. We certainly don't want to alarm you, sir. It's important for us to be thorough."

"Yes, I understand. Thank you."

"Sir, we have to search Lisa's room. That will include her computer if she has one here."

"Sure, that's not a problem. But, she doesn't have a computer here. She keeps hers in her dorm room at college."

"We'll take care of that when we get down there." Jack was reading from notes in his notebook. "We'll also need your telephone bill for the time period that Lisa's been here."

"Alright," The Mayor didn't appear surprised by these requests.

"Sir, did you give Lisa any credit cards or did she have those on her own?"

"I'm not sure she had anything like that on her own. We didn't want her to work while in school so we gave her a credit and gas card. She also had an ATM card that accessed a slush account that we funded. She paid her own phone bill."

"Was there much in the slush account? And did she have access to any large sums?"

"The account wasn't much, a few hundred dollars for groceries or what have you. Lisa was trustworthy and never abused the money issue. We could trust her." He said it with a shrug.

"Sir, could you get the statements of those credit cards now? That way, Casey can get started immediately on checking the accounts."

"Sure, I keep those records in the office here. I'll be back in a moment." The Mayor quickly walked out, and returned within minutes. He handed Casey four folders, each containing monthly statements. Obviously, the Mayor kept his documents well organized.

"Sir, would it be alright if I use your telephone?" Casey asked.

"Absolutely, detective, anything you need. Please, help yourself."

"Thank you." Casey carried the folders to the phone on the wall, glancing through the first one for the service number. They would track the cards for any use since the time of the murder. With the statements there he had past activity.

Jack made a note to run a credit check on Lisa to see if she had any other credit issues that she didn't share with her parents.

When Casey finished his calls he came back to the table. Jack was already standing. "Okay, sir, we'll get started in Lisa's room if that's not a problem."

"Sure. This way gentlemen," The Mayor led the detectives up the stairs.

Lisa's room was full of pictures from high school. It was obvious she had decorated it on her own, and her parents had kept it that way since she left for college. A small table with a mirror sat near a twin bed with a pastel colored comforter. Matching pillows were neatly placed at the head of the bed. A small stuffed bunny rabbit leaned against the pillows. There were a few boxes full of magazines, yearbooks and other knickknacks in the closet. Prom dresses and cheerleader uniforms hung, wrapped in plastic, obviously dry-cleaned then stored.

Jack looked at the matching nightstands on each side of the bed. He didn't see a telephone.

"Sir, did Lisa have her own phone in this room?"

"No, when she was younger and lived with us, her mother and I didn't allow her to have her own telephone." The Mayor's voice trailed off.

Jack had heard that failing voice many times on other cases—it was the sound of losing a child. Right now the Mayor regretted ever denying his daughter anything during her short life.

"I can certainly understand that, sir." Jack gave the Mayor a small polite, comforting smile.

Jack's compassion was genuine. The Mayor gave a slight, reflexive smile.

Jack noticed a suitcase against the wall. The zippered side pouches were open and it appeared that the bag was empty.

"Would that be Lisa's bag, sir?" Jack asked, pointing.

"Yes, I think she unpacked it though. She hated living out of a suitcase."

"Alright, we'll have to take a closer look at her things now if you don't mind." Jack's hand was open and he gestured towards the door. It was the subtlest of dismissals so he and Casey could get to work.

"I wish there was more I could do," Mayor Russell said. "If you gentlemen need anything at all, please let me know. I'll be right downstairs. Take your time."

As the Mayor left Jack wondered what it must feel like to leave men behind so they could examine your daughter's most private possessions. He felt a shiver, then went to work.

Casey started with the suitcase. He found a few clothing items and a small men's shaving bag with Lisa's overnight stuff. There were makeup items: toothpaste, toothbrush, hairbrush, dental floss and a plastic circular container with the remaining monthly dosage of birth control pills.

"Jack, take a look," Casey held up the pill container so Jack could see. He didn't advertise his find out loud. Casey knew the Mayor didn't need to learn his daughter had been sexually active from some loud-mouthed detective.

The job didn't take long, and to a layman's eyes they didn't find much, but in truth they found plenty. Both men were well on their way to intimately familiarizing themselves with a young lady they had never met.

They walked back down to the kitchen. The Mayor was already standing, having heard their footsteps.

"Sir, we're finished for now. Is there anything you might like to ask us?"

"Well, what's next? I mean, do you have any idea what happened to my daughter? Or who might have done this?"

"It's early sir. We have a huge number of resources on this case."

"I just can't understand. Why? How could someone do this to Lisa?"

"Sir, we won't give up on this case until it's completely resolved."

Jack knew the Mayor needed a reason. Any reason would be better than never knowing at all. Someone had to be responsible. He needed someone to blame... someone to hate.

"Casey and I will be heading for Santa Barbara tonight. We're going to do some follow-up down there while the other detectives continue work up here."

"Yes, we were told that the other night at the police station. I don't remember if I mentioned it, but Lisa had a roommate named Julie Anderson. She's called us a couple of times. I think she'll be the biggest help. Lisa and Julie were very close."

Jack made a note in his book. Julie Anderson

would be the first person they met in Santa Barbara.

Jack and Casey drove back to the station to brief Richards. After that they would load up some clothes and head south. Santa Barbara was about six hours away. They would make good time while driving at night. In the morning they would search Lisa's dorm room, then interview her friends.

Jack thought about the stuffed bunny rabbit on Lisa's pillow at her parent's house. *Time to start learning what she did as an adult,* he thought. *We've left her childhood behind.*

TEN

Jack and Casey spent most of the night going over the game plan with Richards. They decided to get a few hours rest then head out at the crack of dawn. The drive south was a breeze. As they got further into southern California Jack was shocked. It had been some time since he'd gone that route, and he couldn't believe the number of new vineyards. They consumed miles upon miles of rolling hills from the southern end of the Monterey Peninsula to the base of the coastal mountains northeast of Santa Barbara. "I remember when these hills were full of steers and vegetable crops," Jack said.

Casey laughed. "Is that right? It's always been wine country to me. I've never seen it any other way."

"The Golden Crop for the Golden State-- grapes."

Jack enjoyed the gradual climb into the coastal mountains. He'd done the drive many times during his college years at Cal-Poly in San Luis Obispo. The highway lulled him into slumber as it wound up to the summit, then suddenly the great Pacific appeared. It spread below them, its blue waters stretching as far as the eye could see.

"Look at this view Casey. I'd forgotten how beautiful it is." Jack paused. "This always makes me think of Charlton Heston playing Moses, standing at the Red Sea just before he parts the water." Jack raised his hands, gazing through the windshield at the view.

"I don't know if I saw that movie," said Casey, his eyes on the road.

"Ahh, forget it. You were just a kid."

They fell silent and the road dove down the steep ocean side of the mountain into Santa Barbara. Unlike San Francisco, Santa Barbara is squeezed onto the beach between the ocean and steep mountains. The mountains protect the valley from the sea. The Pacific there is vastly different from the Pacific that wraps under the Golden Gate. It's a deep clear blue. Oilrig platforms with flames burning like torches lie out in the distance. Even the waves are different. They don't crash onto rocks like they do up north. They roll in and wash across long sandy beaches.

Santa Barbara had grown since Jack's last visit, but the college town beach atmosphere still lingered like ocean mist. Parking was plentiful at the admissions building. The Dean looked younger than Jack imagined, prettier too. His college dean had been an elderly, stuffy bureaucrat.

"Hello gentlemen, I'm Victoria Hall. We spoke on the phone." She extended her hand. She wore her jet black hair straight, setting off her soft white skin. Her glasses with their stylish tortoise-shell frames gave her a sexy intellectual look. A mid-thigh skirt and medium heels displayed her tan athletic calves.

Jack shook her hand and smiled. "Hello, Victoria, I'm Jack. This is my partner, Casey Ford. I believe you spoke with Andrew from our office?"

Victoria's handshake was firm, but her long fingers felt bony and cold. She moved with efficiency, and wasn't shy—the manner of a CEO. Jack wasn't sure why, but he couldn't help feeling he was tardy for something.

"Please sit down, detectives."

They followed her direction and took the wooden chairs in front of the desk. The chair backs were completely upright forcing them to sit straighter. Victoria sat, perfect posture, on the edge of her large leather swivel chair.

She rolled the chair forward, and picked up a folder off her desktop. "Here are Lisa's records."

Jack thought it interesting that she didn't offer it to either him or Casey. She wanted to see which one would take it. Jack reached across. Victoria smiled, gave it to him, and turned her chair slightly his way. She'd identified her audience.

"There's not much there," she said. "Just her application, standard emergency contact information, parking permit, transcripts and her dorm records."

As Jack went through the papers, Casey asked: "Ma'am, has Lisa's room been secured?"

"Yes." Victoria turned to him, slightly surprised, suddenly uncertain of the hierarchy she'd thought she had detected here. "I secured it the night I was notified of Lisa's death. I made a note on the file. Also, I had the janitorial staff change the lock on her door, just in case."

Jack looked up from the folder. "Great, thank you. How about Julie Anderson? What's her situation now? And, how is she doing?"

"She's hanging in there. I moved her into another room and she seems to be coping fairly well, considering the circumstances." Victoria spoke with the efficient compassion of a bureaucrat. "I'll have her brought here, or you gentlemen can interview her in her dorm. Let me know which you prefer, and I will make the arrangements.

Jack wondered if Victoria was at all troubled by Lisa's murder. It seemed as if it might be just another opportunity for her to showcase her organizational prowess to a new audience.

"Thank you. Perhaps it would be best to speak to her privately in here, afterwards." Jack smiled, but the firmness in his tone made clear that this was not a suggestion. Victoria's eyes flared, but she quickly regained her composure. Still, Jack observed that her sexiness had drained away. Jack stood. "If you don't mind, we'll take a look at Lisa's room now."

Casey stood too.

"Of course," Victoria said, pushing her chair back, as she opened the top drawer of her desk and grabbed a single key. She rounded her desk, and took the lead towards her office door.

"Follow me gentlemen, I'll show you the way."

They followed through the main area of the administration building. Victoria breezed past the secretary at the desk, snapping: "Please locate Julie

Anderson. I'll let you know when we would like to have her brought into the office." Victoria didn't even miss a step.

"Yes ma'am."

Jack noticed the woman at the desk didn't bother to take her eyes off her work. He felt sorry for her, and he glanced ahead at Victoria, thinking: *She must be a real joy to have for a boss.*

They walked silently across the campus. Some students noticed the cops, but none seemed interested. The dorm was four stories tall and generic. Lisa lived on the third floor. Victoria unlocked the door and swung it open without stepping into the room. She left the key in the lock.

"Thank you Victoria, we'll meet you back at your office as soon as we finish. It shouldn't be too long, there's not a lot here." Jack smiled. It was his way of politely dismissing her.

"Are you sure I can't be of assistance here?" she asked, practically tapping her foot.

Casey was already inside.

Jack kept the smile, but took a firm hold of the door, with her on the outside. "Oh, no thank you. We'll take it from here. You've been a great help." Jack turned away, cutting eye contact, and gently closed the door. They heard Victoria's curt footsteps grow distant then disappear.

"A real charmer, huh?" Jack said. "She reminds me of an ex-girlfriend."

Casey nodded. "We'll give her a few minutes to get back to her building. Then, I'll get the camera and evidence kit from the car." He looked out the window and saw the dean walking quickly across the open quad.

Jack had trouble photographing the room. It was small, and no matter where he stood he couldn't get a good overall shot. Casey set the box of packaging materials in the center, put on a pair of latex gloves and searched through the dresser drawer next to Lisa's bed. Jack did the work on Lisa's desk and files. This wasn't a hunt for a particular item, just anything that might tell them about her life. Who was this girl? Where she might go, with whom? What kind of guy did she prefer? or gal for that matter? They looked for notes, letters, phonebooks or a planner.

"Casey, take a look at these photos."

"What are they?"

"Friends, I'd guess, from the way they're hanging on one another."

Casey looked. Most of the settings were bars and beaches—people laughing and being silly. *Girls like her have a pretty nice life*, he thought.

"Here are some with her parents," Jack passed on more photos. "You know what stands out most to me, Casey?"

"What?"

"The common thread in every picture is Lisa's beautiful smile. It's sad."

Casey nodded.

Jack put the items into paper bags, and these went into a box. Andrew would examine them later. Lisa's laptop screensaver was sailboats in San Francisco Bay. Jack switched it off, unplugged it, and boxed it along with its attachments.

"The High Tech Unit'll mirror the hard drive and blast through her password."

"They blast through her password?" Casey said, curious.

"Most day-to-day computer users don't have elaborate security, so its not that hard."

Casey found a small CD player with a built-in radio. He turned on the radio and heard rock n' roll. Thumbing through a stack of CD's he noticed something. "All the music is rock, blues or hip-hop dance. No country western."

"That figures. Andrew said the car radio was set to a country station, but it wasn't a pre-set."

"Exactly. Back to the cowboy theory."

Jack rifled the drawers of her desk. "Not much here. A few scraps of paper about classes, knickknacks..."

"You're right; she wasn't a collector."

"How could she be? Living in these tight quarters?"

Casey finished searching the closet and her clothes. "I don't see a lot that might link the case to here."

"Naa, me neither. Maybe we'll get something out of the photos or her computer, but I've got a feeling everything happened up in our city." They peeled off their gloves and tossed them into the box. They took another glance around, nodded to one another and left the room. Casey carried the box to the car.

Jack pulled the photos from the box before closing the trunk. "Maybe Julie can fill us in on some of the people in these." He slipped them into his jacket pocket.

Victoria was at her desk, typing at her computer when they walked in. She stopped typing, but didn't bother to stand. She seemed to be expecting a progress report.

"We're all set with the room, thanks." Jack looked at the wooden chair with dread. It had stiffened his back. He hesitated. "Is there someplace more comfortable we can use to talk to Julie?"

"Absolutely," Victoria picked up her phone, and pressed a button. "Please have Julie brought to the senior staff conference room. We'll meet her there." Victoria hung up the phone without waiting for a response. "Follow me gentlemen." The two men had to trot to keep up. They followed her down a corridor lined with framed photos— staff dating back decades. The senior staff conference room looked like a corporate war room. A large dark, highly polished table was surrounded with comfortable leather chairs. Aromas of leather and finished wood mingled. A refreshment table stood in one corner. Victoria turned up the lighting. She was a quick study, and this time she didn't embarrass herself by assuming she would be present.

"Julie will be in shortly. Let me know if there is anything else I can do for you. I'll be in my office."

"Thank you. We appreciate all the help you've given

us."

Jack pulled out a leather chair. This was a lot better. Casey sat next to him, and took his notebook and a small tape recorder from his coat pocket. He placed them on the table.

A young woman knocked at the door even though it was standing open. "Hello, I'm Julie. I think you want to talk to me?" Her voice cracked. She hadn't had much experience talking with police.

Jack got up first. "Hello Julie, My name is Jack Paige and this is my partner Casey Ford,"

"Yes, it's nice... I mean it's nice to meet you." She spoke softly.

"I'm very sorry we have to talk about this at such an early time, but, you understand it's very important." Jack gestured Julie to sit down. "We're detectives from San Francisco."

"I know. Lisa's father said you were coming. I've been trying to help them as much as possible. We talked on the phone a few times. I guess, I'll meet him...at the services."

Jack sensed she was accepting it. "Julie, we want to talk to you about Lisa. About her life. The things she liked to do." Jack picked up the tape recorder. "We would also like to tape record if you don't mind."

Julie looked puzzled. Before she could ask, Jack explained. "It's standard in these types of cases."

"Alright, I don't mind. Do you have any idea who did this?"

"Not yet. We're doing everything we can. It's very early in the investigation. These things take time." Jack started the recorder and placed it back on the table.

"What can you tell us about Lisa? How long have you known one another?"

"Well, we both started school last year. The school paired us up to share a dorm room. I guess they thought we were compatible." Julie smiled shyly and looked down. She tucked a lock of auburn hair behind her left ear and shrugged.

Jack realized that he'd already seen Julie, mostly in blue jeans, a sweatshirt and scuffed brown work boots. That's what she'd been wearing in the photos they'd found in the dorm room. She'd been in a lot of them.

Casey took notes while Jack talked.

"Julie, are you from this area?" He was sizing her up, automatically trying to figure her out so he could tailor the interview to reflect her values.

"Kind of. Actually, I'm from Paso Robles. My family owns a winery. I guess my parents are farmers if you really think about it." Her cute shy smile shone again.

The mention of a winery gave Jack an opening. "That sounds like a great way to grow up. Which winery does your family own?"

"Johannis Estate Vineyards. My grandfather started it years ago."

"Wow! I've bought wine from your family... a lot of it." He wasn't exaggerating. He knew the label from stores, restaurants, and the modest wine rack in his own home. Jack suddenly realized this pretty farm girl came from a very wealthy family

"Thank you, Mr. Paige," Julie said.

That's it, Jack thought, *a bond of trust. Just what we needed.* "You're welcome. Please call me Jack. And, he's Casey. We're not real formal guys."

"Thank you Jack and Casey."

"Do you plan to work in the winery?"

"Of course, I love it there." Her eyes came to life. "That's why I'm here actually. I'm studying current business practices in agriculture. One day I hope I'll be able to take over the business."

For the first time, Jack noticed her eyes were blue. And they were beautiful.

"How was it you and Lisa got along so well? Her being a city girl and all?"

"I guess we just liked one another. She really wasn't a city girl at heart." Julie gazed upward slightly. She must have been picturing Lisa in her mind. "She loved sandy beaches, like the ones down here. She didn't like rough coast beaches up north. I guess that's why she came south."

"Is that right?" Jack acted surprised so he could keep Julie talking.

"Oh yes. Matter of fact, she once told me she liked that nobody down here really knew who she was, or that her dad was the Mayor of San Francisco."

Jack's technique was working perfectly. *Bond, then keep her talking.* Julie opened up. "She was a very low key person. She never wanted any special treatment."

Jack took the photos from his pocket and placed them in front of Julie. "Can you tell us who these people are? We're just curious."

"You took these?"

"It's standard procedure. We just need to know more about Lisa. Anything might help."

Julie looked down for a moment, slid the photos closer. "Oh my, I look terrible in this one." She pointed to one of the photos. Julie blushed, covered her face with her other hand and giggled.

"I think all of you look great," Jack said.

Julie began pointing to different ones. Over the next few moments, she described the event in each photo as well as the people involved. None seemed too significant to the murder.

"You guys were having a great time," Jack said.

"Yes we were," Julie's smile faded quickly. She suddenly remembered why they were there. "I can't believe she's gone. Who would do this?" Julie began to cry.

Jack took tissues from his pocket and handed them to Julie. They sat quietly for a moment, letting a little time pass so Julie could gain some strength.

"I'm sorry, I promised myself I would be strong for this." Her voice went high with strain.

"No need to be sorry," Jack set his pen down and leaned closer. His words were soft and gentle. "It's okay to be sad. We completely understand. We'll do this at your pace, okay?" Jack knew if he gave her a little control she would feel better. A couple of minutes passed. Both men remained quiet.

"Thank you," Julie sat up straight, inhaled deeply then exhaled. She blinked her eyes a few times then held them wide open for a moment. "Alright." She folded her hands in her lap. She did another quick inhale and noticeable exhale. She cleared her head like a nervous runner getting settled on the track. Jack thought: *She handles rough stuff pretty well. She must have lived through some tough situations already.*

"Julie, did Lisa ever talk about boyfriends? Anyone she dated on a regular basis? Like any of these guys in the pictures here?" Jack pointed at one picture.

"Actually, these guys are friends of mine. Lisa didn't talk much about guys," Julie said, shaking her head. "I know she wasn't seeing anybody because she was sick of the dating scene."

"Did she ever talk to you about the kinds of stuff she would do in San Francisco? Bars, dancing, whatever?"

"I know she really liked hanging out at restaurants in the Marina area, maybe downtown or something." Julie tried to jog her memory. "I can't remember the names, but it seemed there was a common crowd that all liked the same stuff."

"Can you remember the names of the bars or the people?"

"Neither actually." Lisa looked puzzled. "It was kind of strange. There seemed to be a pretty big group of friends. Both men and women. They always partied together and ended up at the same house parties or bars."

"Why do you say it was strange?" Jack was confused.

Julie tried to put her finger on it. "Well, it seems all these people were close, enjoyed the same thing, but none of them seemed to be together. It's like, there were no couples. They were just a big group. I guess the best way to describe it was, the group was very incestuous, if that's the word." Julie looked at both of them, as if to see whether they had any idea what she was trying to describe. She didn't seem sure herself.

Jack knew the lifestyle, and knew it resisted verbal definition. "Did Lisa ever talk about drugs?"

"A little, but she was from the city." Julie said, seeming to equate drugs with San Francisco. "I never saw her do anything like that. She never did anything like that around me."

Jack persisted. "Did she ever say her friends used drugs, or that maybe she tried them?"

"I know some of her friends liked Ecstasy. I'm not sure but, she may have said she tried it once or twice." Julie shifted in her chair. "She didn't seem to have a problem or anything like that though. Like I said, she never took any drugs or anything down here, never!"

"We're sorry to have to ask you these questions, but you understand we have to. It's very important. A lot of young guys and gals experiment with drugs in the city. It doesn't mean they're bad people." Jack was sincere.

"I know. I'm sorry I got defensive." Julie leaned back in her chair and relaxed. "I just hate to think about that." She looked at Jack directly. "Lisa was a good person. She didn't deserve this."

"No, she didn't. Nobody does," Jack was silent for a moment, but he had to ask the question: "Julie, was Lisa sexually active? If not with anyone in particular, would she have sex with someone she just met and found attractive?"

Julie wasn't surprised by the question. "I know there was nobody specific, but I do know she could get a little wild and have fun with a guy. Especially, if she had something to drink." She didn't add anything else.

Jack sensed the interview was over. He picked up his recorder and clicked it off.

"By the way, did Lisa mention if she was doing anything special on this visit home?"

The question jarred Julie out of her thoughts. "No. She was just going to spend a couple of days with her parents. She said she missed them."

"I see," Jack slipped the recorder into his pocket. "Oh, one more thing Julie."

"Yes?"

"Did Lisa like country music?"

"No. As a matter of fact, I love it, but Lisa hated it." Julie seemed confused by the question. Jack didn't clarify.

Everybody stood up at the same time. Jack put his hand out and Julie shook it lightly. "We'll talk again, later," he said. "Meanwhile, if you think of anything you feel might be of help, please don't hesitate to call us. Okay?"

"Alright. I'll call if something comes to mind."

"Thank you," They handed Julie their business cards.

Julie clutched the cards, and stared straight into both men's eyes. "Catch the person that did this, please."

"We will." Jack couldn't help but stare into those perfect blue eyes.

They found their way back to Victoria's office.

She sat at her desk, busy. "Did you gentlemen get everything you needed?"

"Yes, thank you. We're finished here and heading back." Jack somehow became the spokesman for the team. "I believe you'll hear from Lisa's family about her belongings."

"No problem. I'll take care of everything. I'll personally handle it with her family." Victoria jumped up extending her hand to conclude the visit.

Jack was first to shake her cold bony hand again.

Casey went second. "Thank you, we appreciate all your great help." Casey struggled to smile.

The drive back to San Francisco seemed shorter than the drive down. Both men digested what they learned. They gazed at the scenery. The radio was off and the tires hummed on the roadway.

"I think the whole gig is gonna be in our town. It's got nothing to do with her down here," Casey said.

"Yeah, I agree," Jack paused. "Man, were her eyes unreal or what?"

Casey agreed. "Hell yeah. Beautiful and blue." They smiled to themselves.

ELEVEN

When they got back north they found the mood in the Homicide Unit was electrified and hyper-speed, like the last quarter in a close Super Bowl. Everyone wanted the latest update. Jack saw captains and chief officers he hadn't seen in years. Richards was earning his paycheck, doing all he could to shield Jack and Casey from the turmoil. He deflected the meaningless requests, while steering what little was worthwhile their way. That gave them room to work.

"I've got a flow chart of Lisa's friends here," Casey said as Jack came in the next day. "A few of them are on their way down. I'm lining up some of the guys to help us out with the interviews."

"Good. You handling all this okay?" Jack asked, looking down at an endless list of messages.

"What's 'all this'? Just kidding." Casey chuckled. "I don't know any different, it's my first case."

"So what about these interviews?"

"I've asked the guys to focus on getting background—like boyfriends, girlfriends, dates and favorite bars. Anything else we should be thinking?"

"Not now. Just remember, the key might be right under our noses. We just haven't figured out what it looks like."

"I hear you loud and clear."

The two sides of Homicide are connected by a doorway. One side has the detective's desks. The other has the crime scene investigators and their equipment. Andrew came through the doorway from his side.

"Hi Jack." He plopped into the chair next to Jack's desk.

"Hi, Pal." Jack wondered how Andrew always managed to look fresh. The guy never slowed down.

"Bad news, no hits on the prints from the car, at least not from the database search. If we get someone down the road, we'll be able to look for a match with comparisons."

"My hopes aren't high, but anything on the tape?"

"It's a mess, nothing usable. We've got a better shot at making a comparison with the lifts from the car." Andrew shook his head. "The blood on the pedals is hers, a perfect type match. I'm having the lab run the DNA to confirm."

"Thanks Andrew." Jack glanced down, dejected. "We don't have shit."

Casey sat, listened and took notes on Andrew's update. He said nothing to add to the gloom.

Andrew was the one to give a glimmer of hope: "We got one thing. You were right on that bullet. It's a semi-jacketed hollow point, .44 Magnum. That's a big ass bullet and a big ass hole to match. I got the imagery set up to show the likely scenario for bullet path. You guys wanna take a look now?"

Jack and Casey followed Andrew to his cubicle. Casey studied the poster-sized pictures of dead people decorating Andrew's walls.

"Interesting, huh, Casey?" Andrew said.

"Actually, I was sort of wondering: why all the gruesome scenes?"

"They're some of the more unusual cases I've worked. I like the bizarre stuff, like the ones over there with knives still sticking out." Andrew pointed to several photos of dead bodies with discolored skin, twisted into awkward positions.

"Interesting."

"In that one over there," Andrew pointed, "the woman is chopped into pieces. It's unsolved. How 'bout you and Jack solve it after you put Lisa's case down."

Neither Casey nor Jack answered. Instead they stood behind Andrew, looking over his shoulder as he clicked the mouse on his computer. On his monitor the image of an asexual droid shifted through different positions. It finished in a kneeling posture. With a click Andrew shot a line through the head.

"That was the path of the bullet."

"So our guy was behind her?" Jack asked.

"Exactly. He had Lisa on her hands and knees, when she was shot. He shot her from above and behind."

"It explains the dirt and debris on her hands and knees," said Andrew.

All three men imagined what was happening to her before she was shot. None of their thoughts were pretty.

Casey spoke first. "Was he trying to get her undressed with his gun aimed to the back of her head? Was it just: Bang! He lets one go?"

"That makes the most sense."

"Whether he fired on purpose or by accident, she's done."

"You're right, Casey."

"Andrew, do you have her pants and panties here?"

"Sure do, Jack."

"Would you grab the Wood's Lamp and check them both?"

"Sure, let me get the equipment."

"That's the one that detects semen, right?" Casey asked.

"Yeah," said Jack. "It's cool actually. The light makes semen light up like a fluorescent poster."

Andrew set the pants and panties on the evidence table, turned off the lights in the room and switched on the Wood's Lamp.

"And there it is, boys!" Andrew crowed. "We got semen on the back of her pants." He examined further. "But nothing on her panties."

"So he was rubbing on her and trying to get her pants off at the same time," Jack said.

"I'll get a sample and ship it to the lab."

"I'm glad he didn't rape her after she was dead," Jack said softly.

Nobody spoke.

Andrew turned on the lights and popped the CD

with the shooting angle from his computer. "I'll get to work on that sample." He handed Jack the CD.

Jack and Casey walked back to their side. Several of Lisa's friends had arrived, and were going into separate rooms for interviews. These kids all looked shocked. A couple of them were crying. Though they'd known she was dead, the procedures of death were now right there in front of them: the police station, questions, all of it. The common denominator among them was good looks—just like Lisa. The difference was that these kids had long full lives ahead of them.

Jack and Casey went through their side without even stopping at their desks. It was time to update Lieutenant Richards. As usual, he was on the phone. They stopped short in the doorway but Richards waived them in. Jack and Casey sat down, took out their notebooks, and listened to the tail end of Richards' conversation.

"I realize that Chief... We'll tell the media what we want, when we want... Just like any other case, Sir... Yes, a little more time... Thank you, Sir."

He hung up, and stared at them.

"Thanks, Boss," Jack said.

"Sure, Jack. I keep trying, but they're pushing real hard. Oh yeah, we also got all of Special Operations canvassing the bars with the flyer you put together."

Jack wasn't surprised the Patrol Division was coughing up special enforcement teams to help out on the case. He'd expected it from the beginning.

Richards opened his notebook. "Are we getting anywhere yet?"

"What we've got so far is: Lisa's been home about a day-and-a-half. She hasn't hooked up with any friends we're aware of. We're getting her cell phone records any time."

As Jack spoke Richards took notes.

"She's been drinking. Somehow she ends up in a wooded area, maybe Golden Gate Park or something, on her hands and knees, with a gun pointed to the back of her head. She must have put up a fight, because she lost

109

a fingernail. Maybe on purpose, maybe by accident the shooter caps her in the back of the head. It's one shot, .44 Magnum semi-jacketed hollow-point. We found no casing. She gets stuffed into the trunk of her own car and dumped at the gas station." Jack paused so Richards could catch up with his notes.

Richards looked up and nodded.

Jack went on: "She's got birth control pills, so she's probably sexually active, but she doesn't seem to have a boyfriend. Her roommate at school confirms this. We still don't know motive. Her keys, cell phone, purse, fingernail and shoe are still missing. The shoe and fingernail are probably at the wooded crime scene. We're doing DNA, but that's at least six-to-eight weeks before we see results."

"Anything on a suspect yet?"

"Not from a witness."

"Damn."

"Based on the seat position in the victim vehicle, our guy is probably 6'2" to 6'5" tall. He also likes country music."

"Country music, what the hell does that mean?"

"The radio station in the car was on a country station. It wasn't a pre-set station and Lisa didn't like country music."

"That's interesting. I didn't think country music was popular in San Francisco."

"You're right Boss, it isn't." Jack closed his notebook. "I'd like to get some uniforms out checking the park. Maybe we can find the crime scene or dig up a witness. We're a little thin on those."

"You got it," Richards finished his notes. "What can we give the media now?"

"Nothing!"

"Jack, we have to give them something. If we don't, they'll make it up." Richards sat up straight, his arms extending out from his sides. "Work with me a little on this, for Christ's sake."

"Okay, Boss. How about we release the flyer, tell them we need help finding out where she was before the murder..."

"That's all?"

"That'll be enough," Jack said. "We get the media and public on a mission. Give them just enough to distract them. They'll feel challenged to find answers on their own. That lets us off the hook, at least for a little while. We need as much time as we can get—it won't be much."

"I like it, Jack."

"Also this way, the media can deal with all the psychics and clairvoyants that crawl out of the woodwork."

"Then that's our plan." Richards closed his notebook. That was the cue for the detectives to get back to work.

Most of the interviews with friends were finished up within the next hour. Detectives piled interview sheets, photos and CDs on Jack's desk.

"Did you guys get anything?" Jack asked them.

One detective spoke for the group. "Not really. The stories were pretty much the same. They hadn't seen her yet. One or two spoke to her on the phone. They made plans to meet up with her later, but nothing concrete. She didn't say anything specific about going out that night." The other detectives nodded in agreement.

"Ok, thanks for the help, guys. At least we identified phone numbers that should show up on her bill."

Once the detectives dispersed Jack and Casey organized the case file.

"We have to keep all this organized from the beginning. It's a pain in the butt, but if we don't, it's impossible to sort everything out in the end."

"Sounds fine, I like things organized too."

Casey stopped filing for a second, "You know what bugs me the most about this, Jack?"

"What?"

"The asshole that did this has been running away from us from the second he bailed out of that car, and we don't know which way to start chasing him." Casey stared at Jack, his eyes blinking in frustration.

Jack pursed his lips. *Yeah,* he thought, *I feel exactly the same way.*

Casey glanced down at his desk. Someone had put a written message there from Traci Townsend. She'd called looking for him. Casey pulled her business card from his wallet and stared at it a moment. *Okay,* he thought, recalling the sexy reporter, *it's not that big a risk. I can try something on my own.* A few minutes later he walked toward the bathroom, and dialed her private number on his cell phone.

TWELVE

Danny couldn't believe this. A Nevada State Trooper was pulling him over. Red light filled his rear view mirror and the blinding spotlight waved across the back of the stolen car. Danny glanced at his speedometer: 83 mph. He was speeding. *Should I stop or make a run for it? I might have to kill this cop. One thing for sure, no way in hell am I going back to Angola... or any goddamn prison. If this asshole tries to put me there he'll die.*

Danny had cut his hair, shaved, changed and dumped his bloody clothes before he left California. *No way this cop's gonna know I murdered anybody, much less the San Francisco Mayor's daughter. The bitch deserved what she got. She shouldn't have treated me like scum. Hell, I liked taping her helpless ass up. I liked the whole thing!*

It looked like only one red light but it was impossible to be sure. Danny figured running would only draw in more cops. If he was going to kill this cop, his odds would be better with a surprise attack.

Danny flipped his turn signal and slowed his speed. He moved into the right lane, peering into his mirror to see how many cops were in the car. He couldn't see shit. The bright lights blinded him. Danny slipped his hand between the seat and the console and felt the cold grip of the stolen .44 Magnum revolver. The original owner had kept a box of ammunition with it: twenty-five hollow point rounds. So far Danny had only used one.

Danny stopped on the shoulder, rolled down both front windows so he could hear more clearly, then shut off the engine. The driver's side spotlight on the cop car moved. Suddenly, the passenger side spotlight turned on, catching Danny by surprise. *Shit! There must be two of them.*

Danny could barely see the cop's shadow advancing toward his car. He couldn't see a second cop, or if there was another car behind the first.

The cop called out. "I'll make contact, partner, and you cover."

Danny heard the cop, but couldn't see or hear any partner. If he couldn't locate the other cop he was fucked. His best chance might be to shoot the asshole at his window. Sweat poured down his face. His heart pounded in his ears. He tried to control his breathing. *Shit, this is happening too fast!*

Danny squeezed his hand into the crease of the seat tightening his grip on the gun. He had options. He could shoot the first cop, then get out and try to find the second one fast enough to kill him too. He would probably have to reload. That would be impossible in darkness while trying to locate the second cop. And the second cop would be blasting away the whole time!

Or he could get out of the car without the gun, locate both cops, dive back in, grab the gun and start shooting. His odds of winning that one were slim to none.

Sweat dripped from his face. There was so much crank in his system he couldn't think straight. Then he thought of a third option: Get out holding the gun, dive into the darkness, and kill both these guys. He couldn't decide, and he was out of time. One thing was sure: it wouldn't make sense to pass up the chance to kill the first cop.

The cop was almost to the passenger side window. Danny heard him say, "I'll make contact, you cover."

Danny saw the cop in his peripheral vision. He adjusted his grip on the gun and slipped his finger onto the trigger. He could yank it out in a flash and blow the cop's face off. He still couldn't see the other cop. *Where the fuck is he?*

"Sir, I stopped you for speeding. Please put both hands on the wheel so I can see them."

Danny stared straight ahead. He didn't move a muscle. Sweat burned his eyes. He would have trouble focusing on the gun site.

The cop said, "Hey, partner, this guy is a little hinky." His voice was nervous.

Danny was sure there were two. *But shit! I can't even hear the other cop talking back.* As the cop at the window spoke the voice sounded a million miles away. Danny gripped the .44 Magnum. *I'll shoot the asshole in the face!*

"Sir, put your hands on the wheel!" The cop screamed.

Danny heard the cop loud and clear. He didn't notice the cop unsnapping his holster and sliding his 9mm semi-automatic pistol behind his right thigh.

"Let me see you're fucking hands or I'll shoot!"

The cop sounded desperate. Danny looked and saw a gun pointed right at his head.

"Yes sir. I'm sorry. Please don't shoot." Danny had lost the advantage; he'd waited too long. He placed his hands on the wheel, leaving the gun buried in the crease. He needed to calm this cop down, get him to put his gun away. Then Danny could go for his gun.

The cop held his flashlight and gun, both arms extended. Danny could almost feel the site aimed at his right ear. The cop was semi-crouched so he could see into the car.

"Put your hands on top of your head, now!"

Danny complied. *How do I get a drop on this asshole? Shit! I need a new plan, now!*

"When I tell you to, take the keys from the ignition with your right hand, and drop the keys out the driver side window."

The cop's voice was still serious, but he was calming down. Compliance was working.

"Do it now, very slowly."

Danny carefully removed his right hand from the top of his head, spread his fingers and slightly turned his palm towards the cop so he could see he had nothing in his hand.

"Yes sir. I'm sorry; I'm doing it right now." Danny

reached down and slowly removed the keychain holding the shaved ignition key. He'd filed it himself, so it would work in plenty of locks and ignitions. If the cop saw that key, the game was up. Danny cupped the shaved key in his hand so the cop wouldn't see it.

"Okay sir, I'm going to drop the key out the window," Danny slowly moved his right hand across his body and extended it out the open window. The keys jingled when they hit pavement. He placed his right hand back on top of his head and listened. Suddenly, he realized the cop wasn't talking to the other cop any more. They had to be in sight of one another. Danny knew the closer together the two cops were to one another, the better for him once he started shooting.

The cop put his flashlight in his rear pocket and talked into the radio microphone clipped to his lapel. Danny heard a female voice on the other end.

"Control Six-Nora Thirty-One," The cop said.

"Six-Nora Thirty-One, go ahead," The woman answered.

"Code Ninety-Nine control."

Danny didn't know what any of it meant, but he did wonder why the other cop wasn't radioing in instead. This guy was doing all the work.

"Ten-four, Six-Nora Thirty-One, break..."

Danny heard the woman pause, then say, "Unit to respond for Six-Nora Thirty-One?"

Suddenly, it clicked. *The guy's alone! He's calling for a backup.*

Danny heard: "Six-Nora Thirty-Three, roger, I'll take the fill, ETA nine." The radio crackled then fell silent.

Danny thought he knew what this meant: in nine minutes backup would arrive. But, what if he was wrong? What if there was another cop out there?

"When I say so, slowly open the door, step out and keep your hands on top of your head." Now the cop was much calmer.

Danny turned and looked at him. "Yes sir. I'm sorry sir, anything you say." Danny tilted his head sideways.

The spotlight from the police car was less blinding that way. The cop diverted the flashlight so it wasn't right in Danny's eyes. Danny watched the shadowy figure outside the door. The cop hadn't moved an inch. *Good for me,* thought Danny, *bad for you. Just keep that big ass in the same spot.* How much time had passed? Two minutes? Three? Either way, the cop had stopped talking to his partner. Danny was still unsure: one or two? Guessing wrong could get him killed.

"Slowly get out. Do it now. So I can see you."

Danny carefully took his left hand from the top of his head, grabbed the door handle and pulled. The latch popped loose and the door was free to swing open. Danny paused a moment before moving. He couldn't decide if he should grab the gun and move or what? His body moved slowly, though his mind was racing. He figured four minutes had passed.

I'm dead anyway. Danny snapped the driver's door open with his left hand and pulled the gun from the crease with his right. He scrambled out and simultaneously fired. The gun exploded with an enormous kick. A yellow fireball lit up the car's interior.

"Freeze! Don't do it!" the cop screamed, firing back. Flames spit from the barrel of the cop's gun. He fired in rapid succession. The barrage of gunfire ripped the dark night. As Danny fired several rounds the muzzle flash temporarily blinded him. Gunpowder seared his nostrils. He tasted it too.

Danny scrambled towards the front of the car moving like a spider. His body parts still worked. He wasn't hit. Every time Danny put his hand down for balance, the big revolver scraped the pavement. As he moved around the front his own headlights blinded him. He could even feel their heat. Danny searched for the other cop. *Am I still being fired on?*

Then he heard the cop scream, "Code thirty! Code thirty! Shots fired! I'm fucking hit!" The cop's voice came from the ground, somewhere near the shoulder of the road and the rear of the car. Danny didn't know where he'd hit him, but the bastard wasn't dead.

Danny spotted the cop on his butt on the ground, legs spread and sticking straight out. No one else was firing. Sure enough, the cop was alone. The cop struggled to stay upright. He hadn't spotted Danny.

Danny scrambled to his feet and moved sideways across the front of the cop. The cop was shocked to see Danny moving. His eyes and mouth were wide open. The cop let out a gut-wrenching scream as he raised his right arm. Danny saw the gun in the cop's hand.

Fireballs exploded from Danny's gun barrel, blinding him as he moved. The cop fired a barrage of shots. Danny heard bullets whiz past his head as he dashed towards the darkness just off the highway. Danny dove into a clump of bushes. He waited. *Am I hit?* His heart felt like it was going to explode. His gut twisted, he coughed, gagged then vomited in the dirt. Danny waited and heard nothing except the hysteria on the cop's radio.

I'm not hit. He wiped vomit from his chin and scrambled up from the bushes. He ran back to his car, not even looking back towards the cop. He scraped the key from the pavement and dived into the front seat. While keeping his head low, he started the car, slammed the shift lever into gear and accelerated.

* * *

Trooper Haynes's frantic scream from the radio shattered the night. Trooper Thomas recognized his friend's voice, but he'd never heard him sound this way: desperate and panicked. Thomas tried to form a mental picture but it was unimaginable. He gripped the steering wheel so hard his fingernails left indentations in the plastic. His back went rigid; he shook with adrenaline. His thigh tightened as he mashed down the accelerator pedal, but the pedal had nothing left to give. At 125 miles per hour time seemed to stand still.

Trooper Thomas screamed into his radio microphone, "Control, respond paramedics and fire, code three!"

"Copy, Six-Nora Thirty-Three. Fire and medics are code three!" Every second counted. Trooper Haynes's life was on the line.

Thomas turned his radio up to a blare so he could hear it over the wail of his siren. The dispatcher repeatedly beeped the high-pitched emergency alert tone. She controlled her scream as she called: "Six-Nora Thirty-One, confirm you're hit!" Her message drew only haunting silence.

Thomas and Haynes had graduated from the Academy together. They both worked graveyard watch and covered each other's ass. In 19 months they'd become close friends, hanging out together on their days off. Normal people don't call Tuesday and Wednesday their weekend. Only cops, firefighters and nurses do that. Haynes's little girls sometimes called him "Uncle." Thomas loved that. He didn't even have kids... or a wife.

Thomas was first on the scene. As Haynes's cruiser came into sight Thomas fought the urge to drive in at warp speed. He was scared to death. He didn't want to get shot. His training taught him that he was no use if he didn't use his head. With his high beams on, he inched closer. Nobody was in the lanes nearest the driver side. He stopped a short distance back and watched. Thomas was not going to cross in front of his own headlights and reveal his position. The suspect might be lying in wait. He shut off his rear amber lights so he wouldn't be illuminated when he circled around the back. He started for the 12 gauge pump shotgun in the locked rack, but decided his handgun was the smarter choice. It would leave his other hand free for a flashlight or reloading if need be. He was unsure of the best tactical response. No Academy drill prepared him for this nightmare.

He crept from his car, crouching, with his gun and flashlight in hand. His head spun and his heart raced. A cacophony of voices blared from the radio. He darted around the back of his car into the shadows on the road shoulder. He stayed low, search for a target. Finally he approached the cruiser. It sat, a weirdly lit ghost in the night. The engine was running, top lights were spinning, and the headlights and high beams were on. Both the driver and passenger spotlights shone forward. It looked like an empty carnival ride set in an ocean of darkness.

The smell of burnt gunpowder hung in the air. It reminded him of the Fourth of July. He recognized the angled position of the cruiser as the officer safety method they'd both learned at the Academy. Parked this way, an officer could use the engine block for cover in a gun battle.

Thomas knew his perceptions were off. He had trouble distinguishing time and space. Some things moved slowly in his mind, yet his thoughts seemed to be racing. It was the mind's adjustment to a combat situation. He'd learned about that, but this was his first experience of it.

He sensed an oddity: no vehicle in front of the cruiser. He crept another few feet, then, with a snap, he stood and shone his flashlight inside. No one there. He snapped his light off, crouched low and moved three feet to his right. If the suspect fired towards the flashlight beam, he would already have changed his position. Thomas squatted close to the ground, gun pointing into darkness and waited for gunfire. None came. He became aware of a pumping sound: his own heart. Sweat poured down his face. *Where the hell is everyone? Is the suspect hiding or shot? Where the hell is Haynes?*

Thomas scanned the area, scared to death at what he might find. He moved several feet towards the front of the cruiser, still crouching and alert. The darkness made him feel safer. He saw nothing in front of the cruiser. Then he saw the figure. His eyes locked on the light-colored stripe running down the side of the pants. He saw the shininess of the thick leather duty belt and the combat style boots. It was a uniform.

Thomas felt the sick realization that this was his friend. Part of his body lay in the dirt. His arms were spread wide. His eyes were fixed open. He seemed suspended in a puddle of bright red, frothy blood. His mouth hung open, and full of blood. His face was still.

Thomas stepped in next to his friend. He scanned the area: no other bodies. He knelt down on the asphalt, getting blood and dirt on his own uniform. Pebbles tore into his knees. He holstered his gun.

That was when he broke. His flashlight clanked onto the pavement. He grabbed his friend. Thomas screamed, "Please God no!" He leaned close and felt the carotid artery. His friend's skin was warm but there was no pulse. There was no rise and fall in his chest. Thomas ripped open the uniform shirt and immediately saw the remnants of a large bullet gnarled in the Kevlar fabric of the bulletproof vest. The vest had worked and caught the bullet.

He tore the Velcro straps of the vest free and pushed aside the front bulletproof panel exposing his friend's chest. His chest looked grotesquely deformed. The impact had torn the Pectoral muscle from Haynes's rib cage. The muscle had ripped loose and now rested under his right armpit. Blood poured from under his armpit, then stopped.

Thomas fought the urge to vomit. Tears and sweat burned his eyes. He thought about his friend's little girls and his wife. They were at home, safe and completely unaware of what had just happened.

Thomas turned his friend's head to the side to clear the blood from his mouth. He instinctively tilted back the head and gave two quick hard blows of air into his mouth. He felt the wetness on his lips and he tasted the sweetness of blood. His gut wrenched. Thomas centered his shoulders over his friend, clasped his hands together and started pumping his chest with compressions. He automatically counted out loud. He heard cartilage and bones cracking and he felt it under his palm. After a few compressions, there was much less resistance. His hands slipped from the center point of the Sternum as he pumped. Blood made everything slick. The more he pumped his friend's chest, more blood gushed from under his right armpit. Thomas realized CPR was pumping his friend dry of every ounce of blood left in his body.

Tears streamed down his face. *When did I start to cry?* Snot ran from his nose. His throat burned. He felt his stomach coming out his mouth. He had thoughts of God and he could faintly hear counting. It didn't seem like his voice. Thomas didn't notice anyone else until the hands of a paramedic pulled him away.

"He's gone," said a voice. "There's nothing we can do."

Thomas sat up straight. He was soaked in sweat and blood. The paramedic crouched next to him and put his arm around his shoulder. Thomas felt an ache in his lower back and realized other parts of his body hurt too. He saw a 9mm pistol near his friend's hand. He hadn't noticed it earlier. The hammer was cocked. Haynes had returned fire. He'd fought to the end. He would remember that when he told Haynes' wife and little girls that their daddy would never again come home. Before the paramedic had him completely up, Thomas sunk back down on his knees. He wept.

THIRTEEN

Jack and Casey sorted through endless notes, messages and information. It was critical to look at every detail. Jack knew that it was often impossible to recognize which piece would link things together. A key piece of evidence was there, probably right in front of them. It was always that way. Clues don't arrive in sequence. They blow in like a hurricane, spinning your head around. As the whirlwind blinds you, your gut whispers: "This one! Don't ignore this one!"

"That's the voice you have to listen for," Jack told Casey. "It's the same gut feeling that keeps a cop on the street from getting killed. The courts tell us instinct isn't real, and we can't use it to arrest somebody. Maybe not, but we can still use it when we're going down a blind alley, or when we step into a room and look at a scene. Those DAs and judges are the smartest people in the world. Just ask one. But they don't walk down those alleys, or feel their stomachs go funny as they walk into a room where somebody died."

Casey nodded. This wasn't new to him. He'd heard a thousand cops say it.

A possible breakthrough came one afternoon when Richards called out for them to come into his office. Both detectives heard the urgency in his voice. They came in and took their usual seats.

"This might be the break we need." Richards handed Jack a piece of paper with four things written on it:

Escape Bar
2611 22nd Avenue
Cody Sines
(415) 677-9177

Jack handed the note to Casey. "Okay, Boss, What's up with Cody?"

"Apparently, a busboy was cleaning up the bar and found a small purse hanging from a hook under a bar stool."

Jack leaned forward in his chair. *Is this it?* he thought.

Richards took note, and went on: "Cody is the manager of the Escape Bar. He looked in the purse to see who it belonged to and bam! It's Lisa's."

Jack recognized the sense of elation. The clue was like a shot of adrenaline. He felt lightheaded as his mind spun with scenarios. Just minutes earlier he'd felt the draining exhaustion of dead ends. Now it was full speed ahead.

"Let's go Casey," Jack jumped from the chair. "We're talking to Cody ourselves."

Casey matched pace with Jack. He'd already guessed the plan. *This is the big break,* he thought, *and it might be my break too.* The case was serving Casey's agenda just as much as it was Jack's.

* * *

After shooting the cop Danny drove through the night. Darkness gave way to morning. As the crank wore off his body was crashing fast. He needed to think clearly. He should dump the car, and get a cold one. That was the key to survival and staying free of the law.

Neighborhoods in Nevada were different than San Francisco. Nothing grew as fast. Trees were smaller. Streets were wider and curbs taller, probably to handle the rains that occasionally flooded the hardpan.

Danny pulled off the Interstate into a shopping mall parking lot. He saw the Wal-Mart, the big bookstore and all the other stores and restaurants. The lot was a sea of cars. He parked in a crowded area near the multiplex. That part of the lot would be full until late. The cops wouldn't find the car for hours if not days. He wiped the car down for prints, just as he'd done with the last one.

The thought of that last car reminded him of that stupid bitch. If she'd just acted a little like she liked him. Instead she'd teased, then tried to deny him, treating him like garbage. *Fuck me? No, fuck you dead bitch! I don't care who your Daddy is!*

As Danny moved through the lot, the weight of the heavy .44 Magnum pistol pulled down the front of his pants. He had extra ammunition in his back pocket. He held the gun securely with his right hand. He'd kept his shaved key. It wouldn't fail him. He just needed to find the right car. It would be even better if it was good on gas.

Things would cool down in a few months, but right now Danny needed to head towards safety. His sister in Texas would take care of him. She had plenty of room, and always believed whatever story he told her. She loved him no matter what. But, Texas was a hell of long way away.

* * *

Jack and Casey arrived at the Escape Bar within thirty minutes. The bar was closed, but the front door was unlocked. Jack walked in from the bright sun, paused, and let his eyes adjust to the dim light. Casey was right behind him.

The bar had the familiar smell of all bars after closing: stale booze, dirty glasses and mustiness. When a bar is full of people eating and drinking, it smells like perfume, sweat and hot bodies. The patrons are used to the dim light, and they know what they're looking for. The music is loud, the crowd is louder, and there's not supposed to be much personal space. It's only when the evening ends that lights illuminate the seedy side of the bar. In the daytime those bright lights are low again, and the place is big, empty and almost asleep.

That's how the Escape Bar looked.

A man appeared from a hallway next to the bar.

"You two look like detectives," His hand was

outstretched. "I'm Cody, the one who called."

"Hi Cody, I'm Jack." They shook hands. To Jack the feel of the handshake was unexpected from someone named Cody. It was soft and the hand was small for a man's. Then he remembered that this Cody was a San Francisco bar manager, and it all fit. Tall, handsome, thin, metro-sexual with great hair, Cody's face was an olive-skinned sculpture that never seemed to shave clean. He had big white bleached teeth and blue eyes.

"This is Casey," Jack went on. "We're the lead detectives in the case. I understand you might have something that belonged to Lisa Russell?"

"Yes, please follow me, Detectives," Cody said.

Jack noticed a very slight lisp. His pace was fast and direct, even though his hips had a barely discernable swivel.

They followed Cody through a narrow hallway lined with boxes of booze, wine cases and cleaning supplies. His office was cluttered with papers, receipts and many photos of other metro-sexual people in unknown places. "Here you are, Detective." Cody handed the small black patent leather purse to Jack.

Jack was sure that every employee there had already handled the purse, so there was no need to think about prints. It was the purse's contents that might tell them about Lisa's last night alive. The contents seemed intact: credit cards, identification, car keys, make-up and cellular phone. This was why traces on Lisa's credit cards and cell phone had turned up nothing. Her things never left the bar. Lisa had forgotten her purse when she walked out with her murderer.

"Cody, were you working the night Lisa Russell was here?" Casey asked.

As Jack looked through the purse he let Casey run with the interview.

"I was, sir," said Cody. He glanced upward. "I remember her sitting at the bar. I served her an apple martini. She wanted to run a tab so I figured she was staying for awhile." Cody gave a public relations smile.

"Was she a regular? Had you seen her before?"

Jack listened, noting that Casey knew the right questions.

"No sir. Never seen her before." Cody paused, looked upwards like he as trying to remember the night. "She wasn't alone very long."

Jack paused, the answer distracting him from his search. Casey was onto something. Jack wished he had turned on his tape recorder, but it wouldn't do any good to stop this now. Casey was on a roll. They could always bring Cody in later for a taped interview.

"She wasn't here very long when this very tall cowboy-looking guy hooked up with her."

Bingo! Jack thought. Cody had seen Lisa's murderer. "What makes you think he was a cowboy type?"

"He was real tall and thin. Like 6'3" or more. He drank Jim Beam and Coke on the rocks. We don't get a lot of those here." He said it in a tone that expressed his disapproval of the murderer's taste.

"But what was it about him that made you think he was cowboy-like?"

"He had a drawl, or a slow Southern accent of some type. You know, like a country western singer or something." Cody searched both men for a sign of understanding but got nothing.

"How long were they here, Cody?"

"Not long. Maybe twenty-five minutes. She had another apple martini. He just had the one drink."

"How'd they pay?"

"The cowboy paid, with cash."

Jack watched Cody look upwards again.

The manager was thinking, trying to remember something. "She seemed to get real drunk, almost immediately. Actually, I remember he had to help her out of the bar."

Jack's hunch had been right. The lab results would confirm it. Lisa had gotten a dose of Rohypnol. She was probably nearly unconscious when the cowboy took her out. He probably hadn't even thought to look for her purse.

"Do you think you would recognize him if you saw him again?"

Perfect question, Jack thought.

"I'm not sure. I had never seen him before and I certainly have not seen him since." Cody pursed his lips. "And, I hope I never see him again!"

"By the way, does your bar put any type of stamp on the hands of customers?"

Jack remembered the autopsy. Lisa did not have any stamps on her hands.

"We absolutely do not! We don't brand our patrons, Sir."

"Cody, this is very important. If I send a police artist here, would you be able to describe the cowboy well enough to have a police sketch made?"

"I'm not good at describing people. I can look at a picture and tell you if I recognize him, but I don't think I can describe him well enough to make a good sketch."

Jack noticed Cody backing away. Maybe he didn't want to get too involved in a serious murder case.

Casey didn't push Cody. *Exactly right*, Jack thought. *We might need this guy to look at some photos, if and when we get the cowboy identified.*

"Cody, do you have any video surveillance of the bar?"

"No. We have no video anywhere inside or outside of this establishment."

"Is there anyone else who may have seen Lisa or this man together? Employees? Regular customers?"

"I don't think so. I've asked every employee whether or not they remembered the couple, or if they had seen them before. The answer was no. It makes sense. She sat at the bar, and I was the only person to serve them."

"Picture yourself there again. Try to remember, were there any regular customers sitting near Lisa or the cowboy?"

"I don't remember any. It was pretty early. I think she got here around 9:30. The cowboy guy came in right behind her and they were out of here by 10:30, if not 10 o'clock."

Jack thought Cody would be great witness someday, if he ever got the chance.

"Okay, Cody, tell me as exactly as you can everything you can remember about the cowboy." Casey took out his notebook.

Cody looked upward again, his habit when he was thinking. "Like I said: tall and thin. He maybe weighed one hundred and eighty-five pounds. His face was thin, kind of sunken-in cheeks. Like someone on methamphetamines or something. Maybe a crack addict or speed freak. You know what I mean, right?"

Casey nodded without interrupting.

"I really don't remember his clothes other than he wore tight Wranglers or something like them. I don't see a lot of Wranglers in the city."

Jack noticed Cody's comments about the jeans.

"What else can you remember, Cody?"

"Really, that's all. Hey man, I was busy that night. I was tending bar alone. You know what I mean? I'm surprised, I mean, I'm even shocked that I can remember everything I told you. Are we about done?"

"Not quite, Cody, what did he look like? Hair, face... that sort of thing."

"Light sandy hair. Fairly long and wavy. I think it was past his collar. I remember a mustache. It wasn't very bushy."

"How old did he look?"

"Oh, I think he was early-to-mid-thirties. His skin looked ruddy—maybe too much sun or drugs. Maybe both. He was probably younger than he actually looked."

"Thanks Cody, we're about done. You got anything, Jack?"

"No, you got it all, Casey." Jack smiled at Cody.

Casey got Cody's personal information so they could easily contact him in the future.

* * *

Danny drove southbound in the newly stolen, medium-sized SUV. His shaved key worked perfectly. There were hundreds to choose from in the lot and thousands on the road. He was lucky enough to steal one with a child's car seat strapped in the back. The child's seat was a great cover. If a cop bothered to look at him, it would lower any suspicions.

Danny didn't know what year the stolen SUV was, but before he left the lot, he found a similar model. Using his pocketknife he took out the screws, and swiped the front plate. Most people don't notice their front license plate missing so it can take forever before they report it stolen. In the business this is known as a "cold plate."

Danny drove to a Quick Stop, bought a caffeine soda and a tube of Super Glue. He drove to a secluded area a short distance from the highway and pulled over. His hands were shaky. He took the front plate from the stolen SUV, bent it in half, and ditched it in the bushes. He removed the rear plate from his SUV and sat back in the driver seat. He needed refreshment.

Danny opened his soda and took a sip. The drink was cool and the can stung his chapped lips. The fizzle burned his raw throat. He felt it travel down his pipes into his empty stomach. He took a small paper packet from his pocket and opened it. He didn't want to spill a speck of his golden treasure. The yellowish-white powder had a combination dirty sock/chemical aroma. Danny loved the smell of crank. He snorted a heavy line, squeezing his eyes shut. The crank fried his nasal passages. The burn was a small price to pay. He loved the feel and taste as the crank dripped from his nasal passages into the back of his throat. The burning eased and a sweet euphoric high warmed his entire body.

Danny sat for a few moments, enjoying the high. The tingling subsided. He felt good, alert and back in his game. He used his pocketknife to carefully remove the month-and-year stickers from the rear license plate of the hot SUV. He opened the tube of Super Glue and put a few drops on the back of each sticker. Moving quickly, with no wasted motion, he glued them into position on the cold plate. He'd manufactured many cold plates in his life. He ditched the other plate in other bushes away from the first one, then put the cold plate on the rear of the hot SUV.

Danny pulled onto a southbound lane of the highway. His hot SUV had a full tank and a very cold plate. His registration was current. If the cops ran the plate, it wouldn't be likely to come up stolen. The vehicle description matched too. It even had plenty of his favorite music. Danny popped in a CD and started to sing along with Waylon and Willie: "Mamas, don't let your babies grow up to be cowboys."

FOURTEEN

The metal cell door opened and Justin loomed in the doorway. His twisted smile didn't mask his anger or true desires. Kyle's eyes were still swollen nearly shut from the last beating but he could clearly see his enemy. Kyle didn't move from the bed. *Now what? This asshole gonna get on me again? He gonna rub me, beat me or what?* Kyle didn't say a word.

The shackling chains in Justin's right hand clanged together. Justin threw the chains on the floor near the cot. "Get up and strip off them clothes, one piece at a time." Justin smiled, loving it.

Kyle got up slowly. Every muscle in his body was bruised and beaten. His aches sharpened as he stood. He felt light-headed and had to concentrate to keep his balance.

"Take off that shirt and hand it to me real nice."

Strip searches were a part of Kyle's life like changes in weather are for a free man. Or they were more than that. After all in the joint the weather never really changed. Any difference between rain, sun, cold and hot had lost meaning long ago. But he still hated the strip searches; they never ceased.

Justin massaged and fingered Kyle's thin prison shirt, searching and feeling for anything concealed that might be used as a weapon. Justin threw the shirt on the ground at Kyle's feet. "Now gimme them pants."

Kyle stripped. With the aches in his legs it was hard to balance on one foot as he removed his pants. He wanted to sit down to undress, but that wasn't his call. He wasn't quite up for another beating... not yet. He politely handed his pants to Justin. Justin searched and massaged the pants just as he had the shirt. He tossed them on the floor.

"Take off the skivvies and hold them up so I can see them real good."

Kyle removed his underwear and held them on display for Justin.

"Turn em' inside out and show me the inside."

Kyle complied, just as he had a thousand times before.

"Good boy, now drop em' on the floor."

Kyle dropped the underwear and stepped away from the pile of clothes. Standing naked in front of Justin, he felt more exposed than ever. Justin grinned and looked up and down his body, taking it in long enough to make the moment awkward.

The next steps were as choreographed as a ballet. Justin barked the orders and Kyle complied. The orders weren't really for direction because the dance steps were ingrained. The words merely set the tempo.

"Rub your fingers through your hair. Shake it out real good. Let me see behind your ears."

Kyle turned his head from side to side as he displayed the backside of each ear, pulling them away from his head.

"Open your mouth wide. Now lift your tongue. Pull your lips away from your gums."

Kyle manipulated his mouth with his hands like a chimp in a cage.

"Spread your fingers and let me see between them. Put your arms up and show me your armpits." Justin stood a few feet away during the visual inspection.

"Spread your legs a little and lift your dick. Now lift you balls. Turn around, bend over, grab your ass and spread your cheeks."

Bending over made Kyle even dizzier. He thought he might fall.

"Now lift your feet one at a time so I can see the bottoms."

Kyle lifted each foot and the dance recital was over. Just like the weather changing, natural, like a downpour, only different.

"Put your clothes on, then shackle up your ankles. You're going back to your cell." Justin applied the front wrist shackles that wrapped around Kyle's waist keeping the prisoner's hands bound tight against his lower abdomen.

When you can only shuffle twelve inches to a step, it takes time to walk the distance from the hole to the cellblock. Kyle didn't care. He had nothing but time. Back in his cell several letters had arrived. *That's what happens when you spend all your time on vacation*, Kyle thought. One letter in particular caught his attention. He noticed the guards had peeled it apart. The stamp had been removed and the thicker envelope paper was sliced and dissected. The letter and envelope had the distinctive odor of the chemicals they used to check for liquid drugs. The guards had been extra careful with this envelope. They had reason to be suspicious: there was no return address.

Kyle relaxed his aching body on his bunk and began to read the typed letter.

Do you remember the old days? We were so young. Playing, not a worry in the world. How did it ever get this way?

I remember that time you hurt the back of your head real bad. It only happened one time. You were pretending to be an Indian. Yeah, that was it. You were an Indian in search of a cowboy. I remember your bow and arrow. You used to run around with it saying you could take anyone with that thing. I used to laugh at you because cowboys always carried guns. Big ones like .44 Magnums. They also always listened to Country Western music. That's all there was in those days. Be safe.

Kyle read the letter several times and smiled. This was the best news he'd had in years. He picked up his prison notepad and pencil and began to write.

FIFTEEN

Several thousand people, all in uniforms or suits, packed the auditorium. The lights were dim. The folding chairs were beautifully arranged to flow towards the front of the stage. On stage left, slightly behind a wooden podium, was a line of ten chairs. Perfect floral arrangements served as a backdrop. The front of the stage was dressed with dark blue fabric. Two fire engines were positioned outside with extension ladders diagonally reaching seventy-five feet in the air and the ends touched. Huge American flags hung from each ladder. These swayed gently in the slight morning breeze.

Irate citizens were already phoning in to complain about the traffic disruptions. Dispatchers were bearing the brunt of the calls. Some people were delayed a few minutes on their way to work. "What in the hell do these cops think they're doing?" asked one caller. The dispatcher tried to calmly explain, but the caller hung up.

The police procession stretched for miles. Police cars and motorcycles wormed their way from the funeral home to the auditorium. All the stoplights were flashing and cross streets were closed for the few minutes it took to pass.

Drivers kept honking and revving their engines in protest. One woman screamed into her cell phone: "What in hell is this? I'm late for my manicure!" She stared at the procession, then noticed the motorcycle cop holding his hand up to keep her halted. She gave him the finger.

The motorcade carried its special cargo: a young widowed mother and two little girls in black dresses. The girls wore bows in their hair. Somehow that was the most heartbreaking sight of all. Along with the mother and daughters were the parents, brothers, sisters, and others who'd been part of the lives of the dead. It was all headed up by a coach carrying the flag-draped casket of a young fallen hero, Nevada State Trooper Haynes.

* * *

Trooper Thomas had put incredible effort into preparing his fallen friend's service. The job distracted him from fresh memories of that night on the highway. Trooper Thomas hadn't slept since.

They'd seen pictures of officers killed in the line of duty when they'd been at the Academy, but neither of them had expected death. Certainly nothing could have prepared Thomas for what he found that night.

Now the job was to catch the killer. A multitude of agencies and hundreds of officers participated in the investigation. Every single cop wished he could be the one to find the killer. Any one of them would have taken pleasure in shooting him like a rabid dog.

* * *

Danny drove for two days straight. He still couldn't believe the cop hadn't shot him. He flashed back and forth between invulnerability and sheer paranoia. His body was powered by fear, caffeinated sodas and crank. He needed to sleep, but there was a lot of highway between him and his sister's.

Once he crossed into Texas he felt more secure. This was a big state, lots of room for him to lose himself, and shake off any leads the law might have. He'd been born here in Texas, and he vaguely thought that should mean something.

Danny was looking for a particular kind of place: a little fleabag motel not far from the highway, and near a truck stop. Truckers like cheap motels. That way they save enough money to pay their favorite local whore, and they can shower before getting back on the road.

Danny's search led him to the perfect spot, a crappy little single-story motel just off the highway. The busted pavement and worn white lines in the parking lot signaled that this was the kind of place where there wouldn't be too many questions. If they asked anything at all, Danny could get by with excuses.

The sun had faded the tan stucco exterior. The last paint job was well over a decade old. Small rusted air conditioners hung from the windows with ratty curtains above.

Danny took his time driving in, and stopped several parking spaces from the office. With sun glaring off dirty windows, it was difficult to see into the office. He could make out a clerk shuffling papers. As Danny got closer he figured the guy was about fifty years old. The clerk's hair was a gray mess, and he had a beer belly.

The door scraped across the tile floor as Danny came in. That caught the clerk's attention.

"Howdy, partner. I need a room for the night," Danny said, smiling.

The clerk eyed Danny. This one needed a shave and looked like he hadn't slept in a week. Danny noticed as the clerk look past him to the SUV in the lot. The SUV had been a smart choice: new, but not brand new.

The clerk looked down at Danny's hands. Danny suddenly remembered the cuts and scrapes on his knuckles. The guy was trying to figure him out. How much time had gone by? Danny's head was swimming in the fading vapors of crank. "Hey, your sign says vacant. You got a room, right?" It worked. The clerk looked up, and seemed to recall that there was business to be done.

"Sure do, son. All I need is a driver license and a credit card." The clerk put out his hand.

Danny knew there wasn't a truck driver in Texas who'd ever had to give this asshole ID. "My ID got stolen a couple of nights ago. I can't do anything about that till I get home. They got my cards too. All I got is cash. You folks still take cash, right?"

The clerk paused and thought about his response. Danny could see the guy was dying to figure him out. *If he pushes it, he just might end up dying.*

"I don't see nobody else in line wantin' to give you 29 dollars, so what is it? You got a room or not?"

"Take it easy, son. I don't move as fast as I used to. Sure we have a room. You're in Room Eight, just around the other side of the building. Go left out the door, and follow it around to the side. You can park there if you want." The clerk's fingers trembled as he handed Danny a room key attached to an oval plastic holder. "8" was printed on both sides.

Danny threw several wrinkled bills on the counter, grabbed the key and was out the door.

* * *

The family sat in the first row closest to the stage. Nevada's State Police Chief spoke first. Like every uniformed officer there, the Chief wore a black band across his badge. "There is nothing more difficult in my duties than burying one of our own family members," he started.

Behind the stage a thirty-foot screen showed the smiling image of Trooper Haynes. The Chief spoke of the bravery of all officers, and the essential support of family and friends. He described the calling one gets to become an officer, and the sense of honor and duty that spurs them to put themselves in harm's way so that others can live safely. His voice cracked more than once. Each time he paused until he'd regained his composure. Earlier he'd taken a few minutes to learn a little about Haynes's family, and now he used their first names. He wanted them to understand that even in as large an organization as this, they were members of a family.

Following the Chief came the Attorney General. He spoke for the people of Nevada, thanking the trooper's family and friends for all their support, and for all they had given to Haynes in his far too brief life. The AG promised to provide every resource, for whatever time necessary to bring Trooper Haynes's killer to justice.

Finally Trooper Thomas spoke through tears. He

commended his friend as a comrade, father and husband. He voiced the things every officer there felt. He spoke of barbeques, vacations and his friend's quick sense of humor. He recalled the funny voices and imitations his friend often did. Those who'd known Haynes well chuckled behind their tears.

The bagpipes shrieked, filling the auditorium with their notes of sadness and death. Thousands stood at attention, saluting or holding their hands over their hearts, as the pallbearers wheeled the casket through the center of the auditorium. Trooper Haynes' body was loaded into the coach for the ride to his final resting place.

* * *

When Sam was in training to become a Texas Highway Patrolman, his officer taught him to run license plates of cars in motel lots. It was a habit he kept. Sometimes he turned up stolen cars. Other times he'd run a check on the registered owner to see if anything came up. It made for some good pinches. Making good pinches and building great cases was fun. Sam got bored writing tickets and accident reports, and arresting drunk drivers.

Sam had run a couple of dozen plates today, but so far he'd struck out. There was one vehicle left to check: an SUV with a Nevada plate. He ran it and it came back clear. Sam noticed a baby seat strapped in the back. *Odd*, he thought. *Folks with a car like this and a baby don't usually stay in cheap motels. I'm not rich, but the hell if I'd bring little Sammy into a dump like this.*

Sam radioed communications and asked for a registration check on the SUV. After a minute or so, the dispatcher advised him the names of the registered owners, and the Nevada address. It sounded like a married couple. The dispatcher followed up with vehicle information including the model and year.

Bingo! The year of the vehicle didn't match. Sam and his wife had been looking at SUVs lately. From that he knew that this one had a plate from an SUV two years earlier.

Sam advised the dispatcher, requested another officer to assist, and asked for the VIN, or vehicle identification number. He asked the dispatcher to contact the plate's registered owner to see if they were missing a license plate.

Sam parked his cruiser near the office door so that suspicious eyes couldn't tie him to a specific room.

Sam walked into the office.

"Hey Earl, I'm lookin' at that SUV around back with a Nevada plate. What's the story?"

"I don't know, Sam. All I seen is a white fellow, bout' thirty-five. He's skinny, dirty and worn-out lookin'. He came in a few hours ago and paid cash for a room."

"Did he have a kid with him?"

"Didn't see a kid. Why?"

Sam didn't answer the question. "What name did he give?"

"Didn't have ID. He said someone stole it." Earl winced, knowing Sam wouldn't like it.

"Earl, how many times do I have to tell you? You have to get ID from people!"

"I know, I know, Sam. What could I do? The guy creeped me out!"

"Okay Earl, what room is he in?"

"Room Eight. I think he's alone." Earl handed Sam the passkey.

Sam walked around to the back of the motel and saw the second patrol car coming towards him. It was Chris, his regular beat partner.

"Hey, Chris. Thanks for rolling over."

"No problem, Sam. I love this stuff. You find another hot one?"

"Yeah, that SUV over there with the Nevada plate. Earl said he's a white guy about thirty-five in room eight. Probably alone, but I'm not sure."

"What do you need me to do?"

"Cover Room Eight. I'm gonna check the VIN before we hit the room."

Chris took cover behind another parked vehicle. He saw the drawn curtains and the faded white door with its metal "8" hanging crooked. There was no light from inside. Chris pointed his pistol at the front door. If the suspect walked out, he would engage him and take him off at gunpoint. The SUV was in the kill zone, and Sam felt vulnerable as he approached it to check for the number. Still he knew that if the suspect came out with a weapon, Chris would not let him down.

Sam got the VIN number, radioed it in, and quickly moved out of the kill zone. Moments later, the sultry voiced dispatcher confirmed the SUV was stolen out of Nevada. She also confirmed the cold plate was stolen, but had not been reported.

Sam and Chris met around the corner from Room Eight to coordinate tactics.

"I'll cover the door knob side. I have the passkey." Sam showed Chris the key.

"I'll cover the hinge side," said Chris.

"As soon as I swing the door open, you go in first and cross right. I'll be right behind you and I'll cross left."

"Got it."

"Remember, get through the threshold quickly. It's a kill zone," said Sam. "We'll have an advantage because the room is dark. I'll blind him with my flashlight. I'll hit him right in the eyes. He'll be lit up like a Christmas tree if we have to blow him up."

Sam called in again, and asked the dispatcher to restrict their channel and send all other radio traffic to another channel. He didn't want to be at the door and have unrelated traffic making radio noise.

"All units, code twenty-two channel nine for an entry." She paused. "Repeat, code twenty-two." The radio fell completely silent.

Sam and Chris positioned themselves on both sides of the door, then moved slowly, so their leather police belts wouldn't squeak.

Sam noticed his right hand tremble when he gripped his 9mm pistol. Adrenaline pumped through his veins. He put his flashlight in his left rear pocket so he could grab it as soon as he opened the door and dropped the passkey on the ground.

Sam gave Chris the nod. Chris nodded back with gun and light in hand, ready. They didn't have to run into the room. Just move smoothly and quickly.

* * *

The cemetery wasn't far. Officers on horseback lined the curb. They wore dress uniforms and white gloves. The horses stood in perfect formation saddles and bridles shined and polished. The bridles had police badges on each side, showing that these were members of the Department. The manicured green lawn was interrupted with headstones and flowers. At a distance stood a large white marble mausoleum, twenty feet tall and as large as a house. It was covered with flowers in tiny cups, and the carved names of those entombed. Several feet above the ground, one tomb was empty. The doors stood wide open. An empty casket cart waited in front of the doors.

Seven officers stood at attention, rifles at their side. A Sergeant-at-Arms stood several paces away. Another officer stood to his side. His white-gloved hands held a polished silver trumpet that glistened in the sunlight. The Chaplain stood, bowing his head. He cradled a Bible in both hands at his waist. Folding chairs waited for the family. A semi-circle of beautiful floral wreaths sat on tripods, their ribbons and banners fluttering in the breeze.

* * *

The door suddenly swung open. Light blinded Danny. With a head heavy from sleep he wasn't sure what was happening. Suddenly he realized it was people moving with flashlights, and guns—cops. He sat up with a start.

"Show me your hands now! Or I'll blow your head off!" Danny saw a gun pointed at his head. Another cop moved into the bathroom and shouted, "Clear!"

Danny's sense of time was shot to hell. The black-out shade was pulled shut and the rattle of the air conditioning unit blocked out noise. No wonder he hadn't heard them coming. Through the fear came one clear thought: no choices. He remembered that he'd left the gun hidden in the SUV. *Probably the best place for it,* he thought. *If I'd had it here I might be dead.*

Danny held both hands up, shielding his eyes from the blinding light. The cop with the gun to his head grabbed his wrist and yanked him off the bed. He quickly rolled Danny onto his stomach and dropped a knee into his back.

Danny grunted in pain. The cop nearly crushed his damn spine. The cop was pumped up. Danny thought the cop was going to rip his arms out of their sockets when he pulled his hands behind his back. The cop slammed the cold metal cuffs onto his wrists. Danny figured they knew about the murders. But then again, if they knew he killed a cop, why hadn't they just shot him? Here, they had him in this shitty little room with no witnesses. He would keep his mouth shut, and find out what they knew.

Danny sat in his underwear as the cops searched the small room. They found dirty clothes and a shaved key. They stood him up and made him put on his pants while he was cuffed. They took him outside and threw him in the caged back seat of a police car.

Two more cops arrived. Danny watched as the younger cop searched the SUV. The older cops ordered the young one around. *He's in training,* Danny thought. *Maybe I've got a chance.* If they found the gun under the dash, he was finished. His knees trembled. His back and arms ached. All he could think about was going back to the joint.

A tow truck arrived. The older cop filled out paperwork and handed it to the driver. Danny was the only one paying attention to the search. The young cop never got on his knees. *Probably doesn't want to get his uniform dirty,* Danny thought. *Come on, man. Miss the gun.*

Danny got the little bit of luck he was wishing for.

* * *

Uniformed pallbearers carried the casket from the coach across the lawn, and rested it atop the metal cart. The silence was eerie as the family settled into their chairs. Other guests sat behind, or stood amongst the headstones.

The Chaplain spoke, "Please everyone, let's bow our heads and pray." He read a short Scripture, and began the service.

People wept, remembering Trooper Haynes. They saw his widow and his two little girls, and remembered the families of others who'd fallen.

With the help of chirping birds and a slight breeze the warm sun gave the day peace. The scent of fresh cut grass, flowers and oak trees hung in the air. A low hum of traffic hung in the distance.

The Sergeant-at-Arms startled everyone as he barked the order. The officers in line snapped their rifles into position, vertically in front of their chests with elbows extended. At another barked order the rifles snapped into shoulder position; pointing towards the sky.

"Fire!" Seven rifles cracked the air. "Fire!" Another crack. "Fire!" The third shot echoed away while the officers snapped their rifles back into position at their sides.

* * *

The young cop nodded, said something, and waived the tow truck over. He motioned to hook up the SUV. Danny couldn't believe it. The young cop missed the gun and the ammo. The big cop who'd busted him climbed into the police car.

"Hey pal, what's your name?"

"I don't even know why ya'll messin' with me. I haven't done a damn thing"

"Tell me about the SUV and the shaved key."

"I don't know what you're talking about, man. Ain't

I got rights? You ain't read me my rights."

"The manager told us you drove the SUV to the motel. Our dispatcher already spoke to the owner in Nevada. We know you swiped it from a movie theater. Your prints are going to be all over the inside."

Danny shrugged.

"The poor bastard you stole it from has to fly out and drive it all the way home. If you show a little remorse, it might help you with the judge. You might as well make it easy on yourself, pal."

Danny thought for a moment. He realized the assholes didn't know he did the killings. They actually pinched him for stealing a car. He wanted to laugh at them. He quickly realized he needed to get out before they figured out what he'd done.

"My name is Danny, Danny Fields," He smiled to himself with relief.

* * *

Two officers removed the American flag from the casket and folded it with sharp, crisp movements. Ten police helicopters hovered in formation overhead. The polished silver trumpet sounded Taps. Behind sunglasses the mourners' eyes blurred with tears. An officer presented the folded flag to Mrs. Haynes. She and her daughters held one another and wept. The pallbearers slipped the casket into its final resting place. Vault doors closed. A final darkness fell upon the casket of Trooper Haynes.

SIXTEEN

When the detectives met with Richards again, Jack could see the pressures mounting on his boss. Richards' eyes were more red and glassy, and the bags under them were getting darker. The hours he'd spent shielding the team from political interference weighed on him, but Richards didn't give an inch. He kept up with every detail. He was in the hot seat, and Jack wanted nothing more than to get him out of it.

Jack had known Richards his entire career, and knew this guy's biggest concern was taking the heat off of the detectives. Richards always said, "When you take good care of the detectives, they put cases down."

"Cody Sines had good information," Jack told Richards, starting off on a positive note. "Casey did a good job with him on the interview." Jack winked at Casey. "Sines will stay cooperative with us too."

"What's next the next step, Jack?" Richards asked.

"We need the Patrol Division to cough up three six-officer teams to canvas Golden Gate Park. They need to focus on the area closest to the bar." Jack wanted twelve, but knew a request for eighteen should get the dozen.

Richards took detailed notes, knowing the scrutiny they might have to withstand. That's what experience did to you.

"We also need ten detectives to hit the Escape Bar tonight at 9:30 or so." Asking for ten was Jack's way of trying to get six. "They need to talk to the employees and regulars, see if they can dig up another witness... maybe someone that knows our guy." Though Cody Sines hadn't thought there were any other witnesses, that meant nothing.

Richards never looked up from his notepad. "We've been tapping Patrol hard on this case. I'm going to ask for two teams. That's twelve total."

Jack and Casey nodded.

"Then I'll grab five detectives from the Assaults Unit. They'll cover the bar," Richards looked up, "That's what you really need, right?"

Jack went on without responding to the question. "We need the Special Operations guys to start immediately. They need to be out there while it's daylight. I'll put together a quick Operations Plan detailing the area we want canvassed." Jack and Casey were up and moving.

A moment later they were back at their desks, both shoving papers aside, creating space to work. Jack saw Andrew coming.

"Hey guys. I got Lisa's purse processed and itemized." He handed his report to Jack. "I processed everything for prints, and photographed everything individually. Nothing of note, but it's all in the report."

"Thank you for working quickly, Andrew."

"Anytime Jack," Andrew turned to leave.

"Hey Andrew, hang on a second."

"What's up, Jack?"

"We've got Special Operations going into the park to try and find our shooting scene. Would you coordinate the search out there?"

Andrew nodded, "Sure."

"Good. I'm putting the details together. If they find the scene, I don't want it screwed up. We need you there to run the show."

"Thanks, Jack. I appreciate that." Andrew beamed. He enjoyed being involved. "I'll grab another Crime Scene guy. As soon as you finish up the plan, I'll run over to Special Operations and get things going."

Jack finished the plan and faxed it. Richards had called ahead, so Special Operations was expecting it. As Andrew headed out the door Jack gave him a copy. "Call if you dig something up."

"Will do," Andrew disappeared.

Lieutenant Richards stood in his office doorway and yelled: "Casey, the Assault Unit detectives will meet you guys in the upstairs conference room." He turned and walked back into his office without waiting for an acknowledgement.

Casey had already worked up the sheet for the Assault Unit detectives, briefing them for their canvas of the bar. Up to then they'd been in the dark. Homicide information was always need-to-know. It was the only way to stop leaks, even in a big city PD.

Casey hit "print" and copies spit from a printer across the room. Casey went over, took them, and handed one to Jack. They both silently reviewed it.

"Looks good," Jack said. "Let's go."

The detectives were already in the conference room. They sat at the oval-shaped table in the blue, ergonomically correct rolling chairs. They all knew one another's names. Casey handed sheets to a few detectives seated close and threw the rest on the table. Detectives divided their attention between the sheet and Casey.

"First of all, thank you all for helping us out on this case," he began. "We realize you have your own cases to work, so we appreciate it.

"Our victim was last seen at the Escape Bar. The address and times are listed on the sheet. She was in the bar with our suspect. He's also listed with as much detail as we have. They had a drink, then split. She may have been pretty lit up because our guy had to help her out the door. Her purse was left in the bar." Casey paused so for those taking notes. "Jack and I spoke with the manager of the bar. His name is Cody Sines. He's cooperative and was also the one that served our victim and suspect. He's probably spoken to some patrons and definitely, all the employees. We need those folks interviewed. We're looking for the usual leads."

One detective asked, "If we come up with something, you want a call or you want us to run with it?"

"Give us a call and we can decide on a case-by-case basis who will run with it. I don't want to get any of you more involved than you need to be. Again, we appreciate your help, any questions?" There were none. "Thanks everyone, we owe you when this is over." The room emptied. Casey watched each one, and thought: *Five more cops involved... five more possible leaks... good or bad?*

Suddenly he realized Jack was looking at him. Casey nodded. "I think we got it covered, Jack."

"Nice work. We need to meet with the Mayor and his wife. Update them and ask if they might know anything about our cowboy." They headed back to Homicide.

Jack popped his head into Richards' office. The Lieutenant was on the phone, but wasn't talking. Jack said: "Just for info, Boss, we're going out to update the Mayor. I'll let his security know we're coming."

Richards nodded his head up and down, and gave the thumbs up sign. He didn't bother taking the phone from his ear.

It wasn't long after that the two detectives stood at the entrance to the Russell home.

"I wonder how they're coping," Casey said.

"We're going to find out in a minute," Jack said, ringing the doorbell.

The Mayor answered almost immediately. "Come in, Detectives." He swung the door wide. "Let's go into the living room. We'll be much more comfortable."

They followed the Mayor through a wide entryway into the elegantly decorated living room. They hadn't seen this room before. The furniture was tasteful, and sat under a twelve-foot ceiling. Jack noticed the coping around the edges. The center of the ceiling was recessed. The doorways and windows were framed in multi-layered hardwood casings. The room held a rich wood odor: typical San Francisco. It reminded Jack of an old formal theatre. They sat on a long sofa covered with a fabric in a subtle green floral design. The low-slung high-polished coffee table held magazines in a perfect display. The Mayor sat in an overstuffed armchair at the end of the table.

"Sir, we're sorry to bother you but we felt it necessary to update you on our progress," Jack said in a low tone.

"Please, Detective. It's not a bother. We're anxious to hear any news." The detectives could hear the fatigue in his voice.

"Sir, would you like us to speak with Mrs. Russell as well?"

"She's not up to it just yet. I'm sure you understand."

"Of course," Jack said, nodding. "Sir, Lisa was at a local bar called The Escape. It's over on 22nd Avenue near the Park. Are you familiar with it?"

"No, I'm not. I'm sorry."

"She was there that night for about thirty minutes. She met up with a man about thirty-five years old. He's described as Caucasian. He's tall, thin and described as a cowboy type. Does that sound familiar to you, sir?"

Russell looked confused. "No, not at all. He sounds too old for Lisa. Why would she meet with someone like that?"

"We're still investigating that aspect, sir," Jack did not provide any more information. "Sir, I ask that you not discuss this information with anyone except your wife."

"Absolutely, I understand," Russell agreed. "Please, just catch the one that did this to our girl." The voice held none of the tones of Russell's political orations. Here he was a grieving father, like any other.

"Sir, we're doing everything possible, and we are making progress. Thank you for your patience." Jack felt his cell phone vibrate. He glanced at the number: Andrew. "I have to take this call, it may be important."

"Of course, Detective."

Jack whispered. "Hi, Andrew."

"We got it Jack! We found the crime scene!" Andrew couldn't control his excitement.

"Excellent. Where are you?" Jack kept his voice even. The Mayor and Casey both stared at him.

"We're about four blocks from the bar, off 26th Avenue, on a dirt driveway in the park."

"Thanks. We're on our way. We'll see you in about twenty minutes." Jack hung up.

"Was that good news, Detective?" The Mayor sounded desperate.

"We may have located the area Lisa was taken after they left the bar. It's in the park, close to the bar, sir."

"That sounds like good progress. Thank you, gentlemen." Russell sounded both pleased and exhausted. He stood up.

Jack and Casey followed him to the door. As they stepped out Jack said again: "Please, sir, not a word to anyone but your wife. It's critical."

"Absolutely, Detective. You have my word."

At the crime scene Andrew had already coordinated uniformed officers to run yellow tape cordoning off the area. Several park urchins stopped their shopping carts, and others gathered on the edges, watching.

Andrew met Jack and Casey at the entrance of the driveway. "We found Cinderella's slipper Jack," Andrew said with a smile. "Lisa's silver high-heel shoe with the thin laces."

"Nice work, Andrew," Jack took out his notebook, and started writing. "Any chance of a witness?"

"Not one that will come forward. It's mostly homeless around here." Andrew pointed at the urchins with their carts. "Special Operations guys are still looking for someone who'll admit to seeing something. So far, nothing."

"I don't' expect much from any of those folks. Hell, we can't get them to talk when one of their own gets killed." Jack grunted with disgust. He'd worked homicides involving homeless, and learned the hard way that they were unsolvable.

"Got anything else in there, Andrew?" Casey asked, nodding towards the scene.

"It looks like a bunch of blood. I'll get samples of course. The plant material looks similar to the stuff Lisa had all over her. I'll take that too, and go through it with a fine-tooth comb. Maybe we can find her fingernail, and if we really get lucky, we might find a bullet casing or blood from our suspect."

"Thanks, Andrew," Casey turned towards Jack. "How bout' I canvas the right side of the street and you take the left?"

"Sure. Who knows, maybe we'll find a witness, or a suspect for that matter. God only knows we need a break sooner or later."

Sooner or later, thought Casey. *Timing... in the end everything's timing.*

SEVENTEEN

Processing the crime scene was going to take all night, so Andrew borrowed portable lights from the Fire Department and the Vehicular Crimes Unit. The lights, which were often used while investigating fatal car crashes, lit up the scene as if it were Monday Night Football. Not wanting that kind of audience, Andrew brought in pop-up canopies with side panels. Those blocked the view from the ground and sky.

Jack finished the canvas with no success and walked over to Andrew's unmarked car. Andrew had the engine running so the on-board police computer wouldn't kill the battery. The driver door was open. Andrew sat with one leg hanging out.

"Nothing from the canvas on my side," Jack said.

"I don't think Casey is done on his side yet." Andrew didn't look up from the CAD (Computer-Aided Dispatcher). "I'm typing instructions to communications. I don't want to broadcast it over the radio. We don't need the media crawling all over this place with choppers."

"Yeah, I'm surprised they haven't picked up on anything from their scanners."

"Whoever is doing the monitoring tonight must be sleeping on the job," Andrew chuckled.

Jack hit the speed dial button on his cell phone, calling the Lieutenant.

"Richards, Homicide Unit." His voice rasped from fatigue.

"Hi Boss. You're not sounding too good. You need some rest."

"You guys put this case down and I will." Richards wasn't in a good mood. "Where you guys at with it?"

Jack saw Casey approaching. The younger detective frowned and shook his head. "We got nothing on the

153

canvas," Jack said, "and Andrew has the scene locked down. He'll be on it all night. All communications on this scene are via cell and CAD. Can you keep the hounds away until Andrew wraps it up?"

"I'm already getting calls," Richards said. "They're sniffing around. I've got it so far, but it won't take long before someone drops a dime. We can't keep it under wraps forever."

As both men knew, good reporters always find a source "close to the investigation," usually a cop or a personal friend. You hear it in every major story in every city.

"We got the call when we were leaving the Mayor's house. We let him know, so we're covered."

"Thanks for that. We'd get our asses kicked if the Mayor learned about the crime scene from the evening news. I'll let the chief know you spoke to the Mayor. Anything else?"

"No, we'll see in the morning."

Jack turned to Casey. "Do you want to call it for now?"

"Yeah, I'm running low. I could use a recharge."

"I'll drop you off at your car."

Jack stepped in his front door and felt his body release tension. The smell of home made him comfortable. The house was quiet. Sarah's car was in the garage, and he'd thought he would see her downstairs, but she'd already gone up to bed. Jack emptied his pockets on the hutch in the kitchen. He hung his keys on the decorative holder, unclipped his badge from his belt, and threw it in a drawer along with his gun. He walked upstairs and found Sarah sleeping. She woke up as he entered the bedroom.

"Hi, honey." Sarah smiled, rubbing sleep from her eyes.

"You're groggy. Been asleep long?" Jack sat on the bed next to her.

"I was tired and had no idea when you'd be home."

"Did you eat?" asked Jack.

"Yeah, there's food in the fridge." Sarah sat up in bed and pulled the sheets up to cover her bare top. "How's the case going?"

"Tough, but we're making some progress." Jack told her about the cowboy, and Lisa being taped up. He mentioned the Escape Bar, and details of the crime scenes. "It just doesn't seem random to me."

Sarah became very serious and looked frightened.

"You're getting that hunch again, aren't you?" he said.

"Jack, don't you see it?"

Jack shook his head. He didn't see anything at the moment.

"He showed her off! She was his prize. He conquered that poor girl and wanted to show the world."

Jack saw sadness in Sarah's eyes. He realized it was the exact look she got whenever she was reminded of the violation she'd experienced as a college co-ed, long before they met.

"What do you mean?"

"He could have left her in that park and taken her car. She may not have been found for days! He wanted her found in a dramatic way, to show he controlled everything. So he put her in that trunk, in public, for the world to see!"

Jack was silent. He hadn't looked at the case from that perspective.

"She was raped, wasn't she?"

"Yeah, it looks like it."

They both sat for a moment, collecting their thoughts.

"So, how's your new partner?"

"Casey's working out great. I like him. He keeps up and does a good job interviewing. He's a little quiet and private. You know, like he was the other night."

"I'm glad," Sarah scooted back under the covers and smiled. "I'm glad you're home, for a few hours at least."

Jack kissed her on the cheek and went into the

bathroom. He grabbed a towel, razor and shave gel. He went to the spare bathroom to shower. The hot water was heaven on his neck and back. He closed his eyes and rested his chin on his chest. The steam slowly filled the shower and his sinuses cleared as he slowly inhaled and exhaled through his nose. The shower warmed his entire body. He felt himself slowing down. But he couldn't clear what Sarah had said from his mind. She was on target. They weren't looking for a murderer; they were looking for a rapist who murdered— *a different animal.*

Jack toweled off, then slipped into sweat pants and an old sweatshirt. Sarah was asleep. He walked downstairs, into the kitchen. He read a few notes Sarah had left on the table regarding dinner appointments and other social engagements she'd committed them to attend. As usual, he would make the few he could. They always drove in separate cars and he had to carry a suit and extra shirts, socks and underwear. It never failed, as soon as they arrived at dinner or a show, he would get called out. Either a new homicide happened, or a lead on a case. He rushed to work leaving Sarah alone. Homicide detectives that still have a spouse, usually have a good one.

Jack found leftover pasta and salad in the fridge. He threw the pasta in the microwave then mixed himself a gin & tonic with two olives. He grabbed his drink, food and fork and settled into his favorite leather recliner. He loved the smell of the leather chair. He clicked on the TV with the remote and started watching sports highlights. The volume was low, but he didn't care to hear what they were saying. He was hungrier than he realized. He knocked down the food and a couple more gin & tonics. It was the perfect medicine.

A doctor had once told Jack, "You know what the problem is with alcohol?"

"No," Jack asked. "What?"

The doctor smiled. "It works."

Jack had been disappointed when that doctor retired. He'd liked him a lot.

Jack woke up in the chair sometime during the night. He clicked off the TV, walked upstairs and climbed in bed with Sarah. Her body felt warm next to his. He liked the feeling of home.

It hardly seemed like a moment before the alarm woke him up from a dead sleep. He saw light coming through the edges around the closed bathroom door and he was alone in bed. His vision wasn't yet clear. Sarah was in the shower. He felt good from rest but his head hurt a little from the gin. He lay in bed until he heard the shower shut off and Sarah moving around. He got up and went into the bathroom. Sarah had a towel wrapped around her body and her hair was wet. She was athletic and kept herself in good shape. She still looked great to Jack.

"Good morning, babe. How you feeling?" Sarah asked.

"I feel good. You're hunch last night was right on target. I haven't been able to get it out of my head."

"You would have seen it yourself soon enough," Sarah said with a smile.

* * *

Within an hour Jack was at his desk with a fresh cup of coffee. Casey arrived a few minutes later. Andrew walked in from the evidence room carrying 8x10 color photos and copies of evidence sheets. He needed a shave and hadn't changed clothes. His shirt was stretched and wrinkled. His eyes were bloodshot with dark bags underneath.

"We finished up about 6:30 this morning. I didn't want to go home until I briefed you guys."

"Thanks, Andrew."

Lieutenant Richards walked out of his office. He looked fairly decent and his suit was fresh. Obviously, he'd slept. "Let's meet in the conference room and get each other up to speed."

Jack, Casey and Andrew followed Richards down the hallway into the small conference room. Andrew set the photos and evidence sheets on the table.

Richards started the meeting. "Andrew, why don't you start by briefing us on the crime scene from yesterday."

"Sure Boss. Here are the still shots of the crime scene. I've got video too."

Andrew stood and spread copies of evidence sheets across the table. They all grabbed copies and reviewed the list of items.

"Everything we got is itemized with description of evidence and exact location. We didn't get a whole lot out there, but at least we locked in the location."

Jack and Casey nodded.

"The shoe's a definite match, same size, brand and color. I found blood on it. It's a match on blood type with the victim. I'm sure it's hers, but we'll run DNA to confirm. We found a large amount of blood on the ground in a concentrated area. We'll check it for DNA type." Andrew pointed to a photo. "You can see faded tire tracks leading to the same area. They match her Benz." He put the photo on the table. "Basically, she got shot in the head and went straight down. There was no sign of arterial blood spray." Andrew held his index finger towards his head and moved his thumb up and down, simulating a trigger.

"I don't see a bullet casing or fingernail on this list," Jack said, pointing at the evidence sheet.

"That's because they weren't there. We didn't miss a thing out there. The .44 Magnum has to be a revolver. I don't think our suspect would have found the casing in the dark if one got ejected." Andrew shook his head. "As far as the nail goes, it had to have fresh blood or meat on it. It was torn from the bed of her finger," Andrew pointed at his own fingernail. "It was probably picked up by some animal, rat, raccoon, possum, whatever."

Jack leaned forward putting his elbows on the table. "Let's sum it up. Lisa goes to the bar for whatever reason. She meets up with our suspect, the cowboy. He drugs her and takes her back to her car. Her purse gets left behind with the keys so he must have used a shaved key or something. The car wasn't hot-wired, right, Andrew?"

Andrew nodded.

"Our guy must have seen her drive up. How else would he know what she drove and where she parked, right? Unless he followed her."

Everyone nodded.

"So he loads her back in the car and drives four blocks to the park. He finds a nice dark spot and gets her out. She had debris on her clothes and hands. We know she's on her hands and knees. The gunshot came from behind and above, so our guy was on top of, and behind her. For whatever reason, he kills her. She dumps straight down on the ground. He loads her in the trunk and dumps the whole package at the gas station."

Everyone focused on Jack.

"We have a few things that don't fit. Or maybe they do?" Jack paused. "The fact our guy knew where her car was parked bugs me. The second thing bugging me is the duct tape. Normally, people don't carry duct tape on dates. The third issue, why not leave her in the park? Why show her off?"

Andrew piped in, "We know from her cell phone records, there were no calls or text messages. And, her folks said she didn't get any calls at the house before she left."

"Exactly Andrew," Jack continued. "I think our guy planned to take someone down that night. That's the reason for the duct tape. I think we got a rapist first, then a murderer."

Everyone looked at Jack, and nodded.

"Has anyone checked the Sexual Assaults Unit to see if there's any case with a tall cowboy?"

"I'll take care of that," said Casey.

There was a rap at the door and a detective that had been sorting through new leads walked into the room. Richards looked up, annoyed.

"I'm sorry to interrupt, Sir, but I thought this was important." The detective handed Richards a letter.

Richards read it silently.

"What's up, Boss?" Jack asked.

Richards looked up at him. "It seems we have a convict doing a life sentence in Angola State Penitentiary, in the lovely state of Louisiana." He turned over the envelope. "It's addressed to the investigators on the Mayor's daughter's case... us." He glanced at the letter again. "It says, 'The cowboy you're looking for used a .44 magnum.'"

"What?" Jack cried.

Richards continued, "'And, she was shot once in the back of the head.'"

All eyes were on the letter, then they looked at each other.

"How can a convict in Angola possibly know that?" Jack demanded. "Who in hell wrote that?"

"The inmates name is: Kyle Sanders." Richards looked at Jack and Casey. "I want you two on a flight to meet Kyle Sanders immediately!"

"We're on it, Boss," Jack said. "I'll call Angola and confirm that Sanders is an inmate."

"You guys better get to him before someone finds out he's a snitch. He's no good to us dead!"

Casey hadn't said a word. Jack noticed his partner was white as a ghost. It was the first time Casey had showed that much emotion.

"You ok?" Jack asked.

"Yeah, Jack," Casey said, his jaw setting. "I'm ready too. Let's see if we can break this thing open."

EIGHTEEN

The detectives took a flight to Dallas then connected to small plane to Baton Rouge. As they flew across Louisiana Jack saw green vegetation spreading everywhere. Wide swaths of land looked like plantations, each with a huge southern-style mansion surrounded by landscaping as well-manicured as a properly tended golf course. He knew that Angola was north, near the Mississippi border.

"These are your old stomping grounds, right, Casey?"

"Pretty much, but it's been quite awhile since I've been here." Casey stared across the row, out the opposite window. "Have you heard what it's like in Angola, Jack?"

"No, I haven't."

"There's not much in the way of mansions up there. They say it's hell on earth in the prison. We lived not far from there for a little while. When we were kids we were scared to death of it."

"Why?"

"Haven't you seen the movies made there, or heard the songs some of those guys write behind those walls?"

"No," Jack said, listening in a way he hadn't before. Casey was opening up for the first time. Jack knew this guy was shaping up into a first-rate detective, but that was about all he knew. Here was a chance to get inside his new partner's thinking.

"It's the toughest maximum security prison in the country," Casey said. "I knew that then, and I've read up on it since. It's still got that reputation. It's one of the largest prisons in the world. Way back in the Civil War days it was a huge plantation. It covers over eighteen thousand acres." As he recited the data, Casey's eyes went dull, like a child doing an exercise in memorization in a grade school classroom. "Surrounded on three sides by the Mississippi River."

Jack nodded to keep Casey talking.

"I've seen horrible floods," Casey said, the life reentering his voice. "The prison gets taken over by insects that eat you alive. They drive everybody nuts. They thrive in that hot, muggy marsh.

"I guess there were slaves on the plantation, but I doubt they had it as hard as the guys there now. There are five thousand inmates in there. It's a city by itself." Casey shuddered.

"Why were you kids so afraid of it?" Jack asked.

"It was just spooky, knowing it was there. They had a death row, and they had executions. The Warden actually named the electric chair 'Gruesome Gertie.' I remember they executed this one guy, and right after they threw the switch his head burst into flames. We heard about it the next morning. It scared the hell out of us."

Jack remembered reading something about Gruesome Gertie. He recalled that it was now the centerpiece of the Angola Prison Museum.

"There've been inmates who spent as much as 35 years in solitary at Angola. Even though I'm a cop, I think that's insane."

Jack couldn't imagine being locked in a cage alone, with no human interaction for a major portion of your life. He heard what Casey was saying, but he also got the message Angola was sending: it wasn't meant to be pleasant.

Heavy humid clouds hung in the air making the approach bumpy, but things were smoother once they landed. Their rental car was ready to go, and Jack was glad the car's air conditioner worked. The humidity was even too much for the defroster. As the car chilled, condensation formed on the windows.

Outside the world was green. Lush crabgrass carpeted every spot of unpaved earth, including the divider on the two-lane highway. Most of the homes on the highway were trailers, and most of these had a dog or two on long ropes.

"Let's get the rap on this guy from the prison guards before we meet him," Jack said.

"I'm good with that. Actually I thought I would hang low, and back you up on this part."

"Fine. The staff should be able to tell us anything we need to know about Sanders—model prisoner, troublemaker, or whatever."

"Either way, the guy knows something," said Casey. "He's already shown that."

"Yes, he has," Jack agreed. "Regardless of how the case goes, we need to find out how he knows those details."

They parked in the visitor lot and stepped out of the cool confines of the car. The hot, sticky air bit into Jack's neck, raising an immediate sheen of sweat. Though the sun had already sunk low, Jack felt heat radiating from the asphalt. They followed the signs along a walkway to the Administration building. It sat outside the massive walls and razor wire. Jack pushed the metal door open and felt a blast of cool air hit his face and body. They stepped into the office.

"Good afternoon gentlemen, how can I help ya'll?" The guard sat at a desk behind the counter, and smiled as he waited for a response.

"Good Afternoon, sir. I'm Jack Paige and this is my work partner, Casey Ford. We're homicide detectives from San Francisco." Jack held his shield for the guard to see.

The guard got up from his desk. "Ya'll's a long ways from home. How can we help ya'll today?"

"Apparently, you have an inmate who might have information about a case we're working. It's a high-profile case," Jack set his shield on the counter and took out a business card.

"Well, that happens in a place like this." The guard's smile exuded southern hospitality. "What's his name?"

"Kyle Sanders."

The guard typed, while looking at a monitor on the counter. Jack couldn't see the screen.

"Yep, we got him, for life as a matter of fact." The guard kept reading. "Murder in the first. Been here 'bout 16 years."

"What kind of prisoner is he?" Jack asked.

"A couple violations over the years, nothing real serious." The guard didn't look from the monitor. He touched the screen with his finger while scanning the page. "He's been in the hole some, but nothin' that's got him extended time." The guard hit "print" and turned to Jack. A printer at the edge of the counter began to chatter. "I believe they're all done with supper by now. When do ya'll wanna see him?"

"Now would be great."

"Let me set it up. Give me a minute." The guard tore a sheet from the printer and handed it to Jack, then he got on the phone.

Jack didn't know what to expect with Kyle Sanders. It was tough to interpret the inmate's expression in his prison picture. Frozen images make people look more sinister than they actually are. That's why the media loves those black-and-white booking photos when they report a crime story.

"The Warden said ya'll could use his office for your interview," the guard said, looking up from the phone. "I'll take you."

"Thank him please. That's very generous," Jack said.

The Warden's office was like any other Jack had visited: large wooden desk, scattered paperwork, reading lamp on the corner and walls covered with framed pictures. These were images of Angola over the past hundred years. The prison had changed, grown. The only thing that didn't change was the marsh of the Mississippi always encroaching, always threatening.

The bookcase behind the desk contained lines of binders and books with titles like: "Prison Reform Act and

Policy," and "Psychological Aspects of Incarceration and Rehabilitation." On top of the bookshelf were family photos, an autographed baseball and a bottle of *Gentleman Jack* with a bow. Directly above the bookcase was a large window. Jack looked out and saw inmates wandering around the main yard a few stories below and some distance away. It looked like a football field surrounded by a white gravel track. Several inmates had their shirts off and were running laps around the track. Men watched each other do pushups, some sitting on each other's backs to add weight and build more muscle. Jack had heard of that before.

From that distance it might have been kids outside a high school, but then you saw the jungle of razor wire, and the guards with automatic weapons up in the towers.

Jack turned back to the room and he and Casey started rearranging the chairs so they could sit next to Kyle. If they kept a guard in the room, he could sit on the black vinyl sofa against the back wall. Jack put his digital tape recorder on the desk. He heard an exterior door open and a guard give directions: "Follow the hallway to the end. They're in the Warden's office." Metal shackles clanked, accompanied with a shuffling sound of short footsteps. The footsteps echoed louder as Kyle approached.

The inmate stepped into the office and stopped. His wrists were shackled in front, close to his waist. His ankles were shackled with twelve inches of length between them. The stare he gave Jack was expressionless. He turned and looked at Casey. Both held their stare on one another. Suddenly, Jack felt awkward, as if these two Southern boys might share something he could never really know—a culture, a background, or just some kind of innate sensibility born from life in the endless heat. Casey looked away first, and sat down.

Kyle had lived a long time taking orders, and it showed. It was there in the pale skin, and the gaunt look that came from a rotten diet. Nothing about him looked healthy. His face was a blotchy gray from old bruising.

Jack thought about what Casey had said about this place. It was obvious Kyle had been beaten. Jack wondered who'd done the beating.

"Where you gentlemen want him to sit?" the guard asked.

The guard was huge, and not so much muscular, as just a big farm boy. Tobacco stained his mouth giving him a hard edge. Jack sensed no southern hospitality here.

"This chair is fine." Jack pointed towards where he wanted Kyle to sit. Jack was almost eye-to-eye with the guard.

Kyle didn't move.

"Sit down!" The guard barked.

Kyle shuffled to the chair and sat without speaking.

"Hi Kyle, I'm Jack Paige and this is Casey Ford." Looking at the shackles, Jack didn't extend his hand. "We're detectives from the San Francisco Police Department. We want to talk about the letter you wrote." With the mention of the letter, the room's mood changed. It was subtle, but apparent as a heart attack. Kyle tensed up. Oddly, so did the guard.

Jack looked to the guard. "Excuse me, could we speak to Kyle alone?"

"No problem, sir. I'll wait outside. Just call me when you're done." Guard Justin Pierce closed the door as he left. He would've liked to listen, but didn't dare. The Warden would be keeping a close eye on this one.

Inside the room Jack said: "We record everything, Kyle." He pointed to the tape recorder.

Kyle nodded.

"Tell us about your letter. How do you know about the case?"

Kyle leaned towards Jack and spoke low. "What I wrote is true, right? Otherwise ya'll wouldn't be here."

Jack kept a poker face. "Are you planning to tell us how you learned the information?"

Kyle nodded positively.

"Do you know who killed the Mayor's daughter?"

Kyle grinned and nodded again.

"I get the feeling, talking here is not a good idea." Jack let that hang in the air.

"I'll tell you everything I know under one condition." Kyle's dark eyes pierced Jack's. "You get me out of this shithole. I'm doin' life. I wanna' do it somewhere nice, like California." His shackles rattled as he leaned back.

"I don't know if that's possible Kyle."

"Don't lie to me, Detective. I seen it done before. You trade inmates from other states all the time."

"Okay Kyle, tell me what you know. That way I can see if it's worth the price." Jack knew Kyle had thought this out, but he hoped he could bargain.

"Listen...I already told you something no one should know. That bitch got shot once in the back of the head with a .44 Magnum!"

"Let's assume you're right..."

"I know I'm right! And you know it too! I don't have time for games. Before he got out, he told me he was gonna kill the bitch!"

Jack silently absorbed what Kyle just said.

Kyle lowered his voice again. "When ya'll ready to know who killed that bitch, you just move my ass to California." Kyle stood up.

Jack was stunned. The conversation seemed to be over before it had really begun. Casey gazed at the prisoner with an odd look, almost as if he admired the sheer balls of it.

Kyle shuffled towards the door, yelling: "Guard Pierce, I'm done talking to these assholes. Please get me outta here, Sir."

The door opened immediately. Obviously, Justin had stayed as close as he could, probably listening. Kyle shuffled past him into the hallway. Pierce seemed as confused as the detectives.

The drive back to the airport provided time to digest what had happened. Jack called Richards repeatedly but couldn't get through. Angola seemed like a huge abyss where no cell phone worked.

"What do you think?" Casey asked.

"We got to get him back to California ASAP. He knows he's holding a golden egg. It's his ticket." Jack stared forward as he drove.

"He said some interesting stuff, that's for sure," Casey said.

"It makes sense too, if it wasn't random, and it doesn't look like it was. I think he's got something for us. Someone Kyle knows had it out for Lisa."

"We can always ship him back if he doesn't pan out, right?"

"Probably not," Jack corrected. "We'd end up with him in California. But I don't care. He's locked up. It doesn't affect us, right?"

"Yeah, I guess so." Casey said staring ahead.

* * *

The walk back to the cell felt long, as if time were extending. Kyle sensed that Justin was keyed up. Was it curiosity? Hostility? Or both? The guard followed him into the cell to remove the restraints, which was out of the ordinary.

As Kyle slipped out of the last ankle restraint Justin snapped. His heavy body forced Kyle against the wall, nearly crushing him. The guard grabbed Kyle's throat, squeezing his windpipe. At the same time, Justin reached down and twisted his testicles. Pain shot through his stomach and kidneys.

Justin's breath was against Kyle's cheek. The position had a horror that had become familiar. "You ain't gettin' outta here boy! Not unless it's in a pine box!"

Kyle couldn't speak. Pain and lack of air left him on the verge of losing consciousness. He thought his eyeballs might explode.

"Them assholes ain't takin' my bitch!" Justin's voice pitched high, like whining brakes. Kyle could feel the trembling strength in the guard's muscles.

Justin grabbed Kyle's hair. The inmate didn't feel himself getting slammed to the floor. He had already passed out.

NINETEEN

Danny had no transportation and just a few bucks left. Not that he was complaining. He still couldn't believe the cops had let him out so fast. All they had on him was car theft, and the county lockup was jammed up enough that a car thief didn't rate a cell. They gave him a trial date and let him go. Hell, they probably didn't even expect him to show up in court. They might have to convict him, then pay for his upkeep for years.

When those assholes had burst into his room, he'd thought for sure he was done, but they hadn't found the gun in the SUV. That was all right. There were plenty of guns around.

Danny hopped on a bus headed east. He wanted to keep moving. He rode the bus as far as his ticket would take him. He didn't catch the name of the town he landed in. He didn't much care.

Danny got off, and started walking around. He found a likely neighborhood right near the bus stop. It was a nice day. Nobody paid attention to him. He searched for a house that looked empty but had cars, focusing on ones with their curtains drawn. People usually close curtains and windows when they leave. Most folks in this small working class neighborhood had jobs. It wouldn't take long to find the right house. Most people in Texas had guns too. That was on his list.

Danny looked at several homes, pausing to listen for the hum of an air conditioner or a dog barking. If he heard either, he moved on. There was a nice house on the corner of a cul-de-sac. From the three sides he could see it appeared nobody was home. He banged his knuckles on the side fence as he walked along. *No barking dog.*

He checked the windows for alarm stickers or

contacts. There were none. He noticed the gate to the backyard was on the concealed side of the house. *Perfect.* Danny walked onto the front porch as if he were expected. He pushed the doorbell and heard it ring through the closed door.

If someone answered, he would ask for a random name then act confused, saying he must have the wrong address. Danny pushed the doorbell again. He listened for the telephone. *Sometimes nosey neighbors call to say there's a stranger on the porch.* The house was silent. He turned the front door knob and felt the resistance of the lock. If he had to kick in a door, it would be around back or in the garage. That would be safer.

Danny moved across the driveway to the side gate accessing the backyard. All the while, he scanned the neighboring houses to see if anyone was watching. He saw nobody. The gate wasn't locked. He slipped into the backyard. The house was locked up but the door leading from the side yard to the garage gave way as if it were cardboard. He noticed a Chevy in the garage. The door from the house into the garage was unlocked.

Danny felt the excitement of walking through someone's house. He loved every minute of this: looking through photos, opening closets, rifling through drawers. He fondled the panties and bras in the bedroom dresser. He discovered a sexy silk G-String, wrapped it around his erect penis and masturbated. He finished quickly. He wiped himself with a tissue and flushed it down the toilet. In the bathroom he searched the medicine cabinet for good prescription drugs. He grabbed a toothbrush from the counter and brushed his teeth. He put the toothbrush back where he found it, laughing to himself.

He searched through every closet and under every mattress. Jackpot! There was a fully loaded, 9mm semi-auto pistol under the mattress in the master bedroom. Danny found over four hundred dollars in cash. Taking whatever he pleased made him euphoric. He helped himself to a beer and leftover chicken from the fridge. The keys to the car were hanging in the kitchen next to the phone. He put them in his pocket. Danny took a piss and tucked the gun in his waistband. He grabbed the rest of the chicken, a bag of chips and all the beer. He noticed a file on the workbench in the garage. He used it to quickly file another key on the ring— another shaved key. *The goddamn cops kept my last one.*

Danny backed the car out of the garage, while watching for nosey neighbors. *No one's around,* he thought. *This neighborhood's deserted.* Danny smiled as he saw the house disappear in his rear view mirror. *My lucky day!*

* * *

Jack and Casey touched down in San Francisco International Airport. As they waited for baggage Jack turned on his cell phone and checked his messages.

"Hey, Casey."

"Yeah?"

"I got an urgent message from Auto Theft."

"What's up?"

"Remember, I flagged all stolen vehicles taken the night Lisa was murdered?" Jack talked while listening to the message.

"Yeah."

"A Nevada Trooper called to confirm a stolen auto they recovered in a movie theater parking lot."

"Nevada?"

"Yeah, the car was stolen ten blocks from the gas station the night Lisa was murdered. They say it looks like it's been there about a week. They want me to call them back." Jack felt ecstatic. He hoped it wasn't just exhaustion, but he was pretty sure this was good—maybe great. The case was breaking open. He quickly dialed the phone number of the Nevada state trooper.

The trooper answered: "Mike Simpson."

"Hi, Mike. This is Jack Paige from the Homicide Unit, San Francisco PD."

"Hello, Detective, thanks for calling back. We

recovered a car from your city. Your Auto Theft Unit confirmed it was stolen, but said I needed to talk to you."

"This is what's up, Mike: I had the car flagged because it was stolen the same night our Mayor's daughter was murdered. It was taken ten blocks from the place we discovered her body."

"What! Holy shit! I heard about that case!"

"We're still on it," Jack said.

"Sir, do you mind if I ask how she was killed?" The trooper's voice suddenly became shaky.

"She was shot."

"Sir, don't tell me it was a .44 Magnum round."

Something in Simpson's voice made Jack's ecstasy turn into nausea. "I'm afraid to ask why," he said.

"The same night your victim was murdered, my friend was gunned down on a traffic stop. His name was Thomas Haynes. He was killed with a .44 Magnum."

Jack felt sick. His stomach knotted and a choking sensation clogged his throat. He remembered when his first partner was killed in the line of duty. Jack always felt responsible. The pain never went away. The funeral was etched into his memory. He still saw the distraught faces of his partner's wife and son.

"Mike, I'm so sorry." Jack collected his emotions. "Now this is important. Are you listening?"

"Yes Sir."

"I guarantee the killer took another vehicle from the lot. You need to check your stolen vehicles from that night, ASAP."

"Yes Sir. I'm on it now. I'll call you back."

Jack hung up and saw Casey staring at him. "It looks like our guy fled to Nevada. He probably killed a Nevada Trooper along the way."

* * *

While Jack waited for his baggage and got more updates from Nevada and Texas, Casey headed for the men's room. Once he was out of Jack's sight he took the business card from his wallet and dialed the handwritten number.

"Hello," the sexy voice answered.

"Hi Traci, it's me Casey Ford."

"Hello Detective," Traci sounded sleepy. "Uhmmm... I love when you call. I'm in bed you know, catnapping."

"Traci, I have something important to tell you."

"Can you come over and tell me in person, baby?"

"It's about the Mayor's daughter's case and I don't have much time!"

"What is it?" Traci recognized his tone, and was all business. When she baited the hook this was what she was fishing for. Now the fish had the worm.

"There's a guy in Angola State Penitentiary in Louisiana, his name is Kyle Sanders," said Casey.

"Okay, okay... I'm getting it!"

"He has specific information about the murder. He says he knows it was planned, and he knows who did it." Crowds were passing, headed for their luggage. Casey cupped the phone with his hand.

"What else does he know?" she asked.

"That's what we'd like to find out. I'm just worried that it might take the brass too long to see this guy's true value. He's key. But, Traci, you can't let on where you heard it, okay?"

"You do like me, don't you baby? That's why you're telling me, right?"

"Of course I do, Traci. But when they start asking about sources, just hint that you know somebody down there in Louisiana, okay?"

"What's next? Are you close to making an arrest?"

"I'll let you know," he said, his hands sweating. But promise me, not a word about me, okay?"

"Yes... yes, of course. I've got it. Thanks, honey."

"I gotta go. I'll talk to you later," Casey heard her squeal with excitement before he hung up the phone. He didn't wait for Traci Townsend to say goodbye. He had to trust her on this one. Hopefully, she wouldn't give him up. Casey knew Traci was a weak link and a promise from a woman like her was as shallow as a desert mirage was risky. Unfortunately, this window of opportunity was closing fast.

* * *

Jack recognized the anxiety in the Nevada trooper's voice when he called back.

"Detective Paige, you were right!"

"Excellent!" Jack nodded and winked at Casey, who was just getting back from the men's room. Jack had their baggage at his side.

"We had an SUV and a cold plate stolen the same night," said the trooper. "They were both recovered at a motel in Texas several days ago."

Jack listened, picturing the sequence of events.

"The owner of the stolen vehicle picked up his SUV in Texas and drove it home. We got troopers heading over to search it right now."

"Excellent! What were the circumstances in Texas?"

"Apparently, they located the vehicle at a motel and a suspect was arrested."

"Is he still in custody?"

"Unfortunately, he was released. They only had him for possession of a stolen auto. They don't hold non-violent felons."

"Tell your guys to rip that vehicle to shreds. That .44 Magnum is definitely in that SUV!"

"Yes, Sir."

"Tell me they positively identified the suspect before they kicked him loose." Jack held his breath.

"They did. Danny Fields is his name."

Jack heard the crack of the bat and the roar of the crowd. The trooper had hit a grand slam: the name. Jack had never heard of Danny Fields. Why should he? But when a name is finally attached to a suspect who's consumed the time and energy of so many people it's like a spotlight suddenly lighting the sky. All the grueling days and sleepless nights gain meaning with a single name:

Danny Fields. "Danny Fields," Jack said, tasting it. "Who's your contact in Texas?"

"Detective Herman Porter, Sir."

"Excellent! Do me a favor. Call me when you guys find that gun."

"Yes Sir, will do!"

Jack took the number for Porter and dialed it.

He answered on the first ring. "This is Detective Porter."

"Hello Detective Porter. My name is Jack Paige"

"I've been waiting for your call Detective Paige. And please, call me Herman." His voice sounded articulate and bright.

"Please, call me Jack. I guess you know why I'm calling?"

"I just need an email address from you. I'll email you a six-pack of photos, including Danny Fields. Is there anything else you need, Jack?"

"Are you always this dialed in, Herman?"

"I try."

"You're doing one helluva job!"

"Thank you. Let me know how it goes."

Herman Porter filled in Jack on the rest of the details before they hung up. The police department was a short drive from the airport. Jack's cell phone rang just as they arrived at the office. Jack recognized the number on the caller ID. It was Trooper Mike Simpson.

"Mike, what's up?"

"They got it, Detective. Just like you said."

"Outstanding." Jack gave Casey the thumbs up sign.

"It's a .44 magnum revolver. The serial number is obliterated, but our lab will try to recover it."

"I'll have my crime scene guys email you the ballistics on our case. You'll have it in ten minutes."

"They also found a box of ammunition. Everything was tucked up under the dash. They were hidden in a wiring harness."

"It's going to match the gun that killed your friend,

Haynes," said Jack.

"I promise you one thing for sure, Detective Paige."

"What's that Mike?"

"It's gonna be a helluva race between you guys and us, to see who's first to catch this son-of-a-bitch."

"Mike, we're on the same side. We all want the same thing. I promise."

"Yes Sir."

TWENTY

Within minutes Jack and Casey were sitting in Lieutenant Richards' office with the door closed. Now that the case was breaking Jack didn't want any possibility of a leak.

Jack sat on the edge of his chair and leaned forward. He looked like a sprinter in the starting blocks.

"Get out your notebook and pen." Jack waited a moment while Richards fished for writing materials.

"Now, write this down: Danny Fields." Jack exhaled, slid back in his chair and smiled for the first time in a week.

"Excellent, Jack!" Richards slammed his hand on the desk. "How the hell did you guys break it?"

"I just got off the phone with a detective from Nevada. They lost a state trooper. They think this scum, Danny, killed him during a car stop." Jack didn't hide his anger.

"That motherfu..." Richards muttered.

"Afterwards Danny drove to Texas and got pinched for having a stolen vehicle."

Richards looked up. "So?"

"Don't get too excited. They already kicked him loose. But at least they positively identified him."

"Texas? Why's he in Texas?" Richards thought aloud. "Sorry Jack. Go ahead."

Jack took a moment to assemble all the pieces in his mind. He spoke carefully. "Lisa was at the Escape Bar when Danny hooked up with her. He dumped a drug into her drink."

"We aren't sure of that," Casey said quickly.

Jack nodded. "Okay, that's still unconfirmed, but it's logical. She became heavily intoxicated very quickly. Danny helps her out of the bar and back to her own car.

178

My feeling is, he followed her to the bar."

"We aren't completely sure of that either," said Casey.

Jack glanced at his partner, not sure if he wanted this devil's advocate stuff or not. Still, the guy was thinking. Jack went on: "Danny most likely went back to Lisa's car to see if his shaved key worked on it. It did. That's why he didn't need her purse or keys. Remember? Those were left in the bar and the car wasn't hot-wired."

Casey didn't argue. Richards nodded while writing.

"He drives her four blocks to the park. He takes that little dirt driveway and stops behind the bushes. He's hidden from view from the street." Jack pointed and wiggled his finger, thinking it through.

"He gets Lisa out and takes her behind the car. Somehow, she gets on all fours, hands and knees. Danny's behind her. He's got his pants down and he's trying to sexually assault her. Remember? There was semen detected on the back of her jeans." Jack paused so Richards could catch up.

"Danny's trying to get his business done while he's holding the gun. He either accidentally, or on purpose, cranks off a round and it hits Lisa in the back of her head. Andrew said based on blood spatter, she dumped straight down to the ground. We know she didn't run around after the shot.

"Danny's a rapist. He wants to continue controlling Lisa. Rather than leave her hidden in the park, he dumps his trophy where she'll be found." Jack frowned, sick at the thought.

"Somewhere along the line, Lisa lost her shoe and fingernail. I think the nail got torn off when he was trying to get her in the trunk. We didn't find the nail, but there was no other DNA on the nail bed."

"That's right," Richards said.

"Danny had to spend a little time in the car because it was wiped clean of prints. So he tunes in a country western station because he doesn't like to hear what's playing. Maybe it calms him down.

"Danny drives a couple of miles to the gas station, sees it's closed and dumps the car. He walks about ten blocks, steals another car and gets the hell out of Dodge."

"Hours later, in the middle of the night, Trooper Haynes patrols for drunk drivers and speeders on the Nevada highway. Unfortunately, he stops Danny. We know he put out the location of the stop because he called for a fill unit. But, he never put out the plate. His fill is about eight minutes out." Jack paused again, taking a deep breath.

"Trooper Haynes comes up on the radio. He's screaming for help and says he's been shot!"

Richards swallowed hard, feeling the same chill Jack did.

"His fill units found him dead on the side of the road, hit twice. One round hit the front panel of his vest. The second round hit him under the right armpit." Jack unconsciously traced a line from his own chest towards his own armpit. "The round tore through both lungs and his heart. There was nothing they could do to save him."

The three men sat silent for a few seconds. Richards spoke first. "Did Trooper Haynes have a family?"

"Yeah, a wife and two little girls." Jack's voice thickened.

Richards didn't say a word. He nodded his head from side to side and pursed his lips tight. His eyes took on a look cold with vengeance.

"Danny drives to a huge parking lot at a super mall of some type. You know? Big stores, theaters and restaurants."

Richards nodded.

"He dumps the car, swipes an SUV, and before he leaves the lot, he grabs a cold plate off another SUV. But he screws up. The cold plate is off a model that's a couple of years different from the SUV he swiped.

"He ends up at this fleabag motel off the highway in Texas. A Texas cop cruising the parking lot figures out the SUV is hot and the cold plate doesn't match."

"Good police work," Richards commented.

"Exactly! They hit up the clerk, get a pass key and take off Danny while he's crashed out, alone in bed."

"Any gun?" Richards asked.

"No, all they got him for is the hot SUV. They're like us here, no room at the inn for car thieves so they kick him loose with a court date."

"So...what about the gun?" Richards asked.

"The room was clean, no gun. They had a training car with a recruit impound the SUV. Apparently, he missed the gun, because the Nevada Troopers found it under the dashboard about thirty minutes ago. They're getting it to the lab ASAP."

"What's next Jack? What do you need?" Richards stopped writing and rubbed a cramp in his palm.

"On my way in here, I asked Andrew to fax the ballistic information to Nevada."

"Good."

"I also talked to a detective in Texas. He's emailing a six-pack of Danny so we can do a photo-line-up with Cody at the Escape Bar."

"Excellent. So how does Kyle Sanders fit into this case?"

"He somehow knew Lisa was going to be killed. Someone in Angola told him he was going after her. Whoever it was, also told him how he was going to do it. It was not random."

"And why did Danny go to Texas? Is he related to Kyle or Angola?"

"I haven't a clue Boss. We're working on that now. But either way, Kyle has some very specific information."

"What's he want?"

"He wants out of Angola. He's doing life and wants us to do a prisoner exchange so he can do his time in California."

"Why the hell does he want to do his time here?"

"I don't know. But it's his bargaining chip and we don't have much choice at this point."

"What's it going to take to get him out?"

"I'll write a quick affidavit on the case and get a

spring order for Kyle. Judge Ambrose will give me the order to get Kyle out of Angola. I'll call my contact in Sacramento at the Board of Prisons and make arrangements to house him at San Quentin."

"Sounds good."

"Casey can use the same affidavit and get a Ramey Warrant on Danny. That way, we don't need to file the entire case with the District Attorney's Office and wait for an Arrest Warrant."

"Casey, do you have a judge for the Ramey?"

"Absolutely, Boss."

There was a knock at the door. "Come in," Richards yelled.

The door opened slightly and Andrew peeked in. "Sorry to interrupt Lieutenant. We just got the call. The media discovered the place Lisa was murdered. That reporter, Traci Townsend is doing a live report. It's on Channel Four."

"Thanks Andrew." Richards used the remote to turn on the television hanging in the corner of his office.

The station flashed the San Francisco Police shield on the screen. It was the same background they used on all crime stories. The letters 'Special Report' flashed across the screen.

The anchor said, "We're going live to Reporter Traci Townsend. She has learned of an incredible break in the Lisa Russell murder. Traci?"

"Don't tell me either of you have done a press release," said Richards.

"Press release? We just got back for Christ's sakes," said Jack.

Traci looked spectacular, gleaming with the inner glow of her secret. She stood with the park scene as backdrop.

"Thanks, Bill." Her TV voice wasn't so sweet, though sex still permeated her delivery. "Earlier, we discovered Lisa Russell was murdered fifty yards from where I'm standing." She pointed. "Just beyond those bushes in the park." The camera panned to the area.

"Even more incredible, we've learned from sources close to the investigation, that there is an inmate in Angola State Penitentiary in Louisiana, who knew Lisa Russell was going to be murdered."

"What the hell?" Jack jumped from his chair.

"We have also learned that the inmate is serving life in prison for a murder he committed sixteen years ago." Traci smiled in triumph.

Jack stared, not even noticing the phone ringing on Richards' desk. Richards picked it up.

Onscreen Traci said: "Our investigators here will certainly need to ask Sanders to reveal how he came to his knowledge of the murder."

"I can't believe this is happening," Jack yelled.

Richards' face was beat red as a voice screamed through the phone.

"I'll handle it, damn it!" Richards shouted. "I hate leaks!" Richards slammed down the phone. "That was the Chief. He's already getting calls. Get that asshole, Sanders, here ASAP!"

* * *

Judge Ambrose was great for law enforcement. He'd started out as a cop decades earlier. He was smart enough to recognize the streets were mean and he wanted to work in a different part of the judicial system. He went to law school at night, graduated, passed the bar exam and got a job at the District Attorney's office. He was a prosecutor for seven years, and then got elected to the bench. That was fifteen years ago.

Jack had known Judge Ambrose since he was a young prosecutor. They'd had many trials together over the years. Judge Ambrose had presided in a good number of homicide trials where Jack was the lead investigator. Judge Ambrose had recognized that Jack was special, that he cared about people and was fair. It made no difference whether Jack was answering questions under direct or cross-examination. He was open and honest to both sides.

Jack had a unique appeal to jurors. They liked him. They saw that he was a professional who did it right. Prosecutors loved it. Defense attorneys hated it.

Jack liked Judge Ambrose's courtroom. American flags were framed on every wall. Some were tattered, others pristine. They represented a collection Judge Ambrose had assembled over decades. The bench was built with solid oak, handcrafted and finished in high-gloss. All Superior Court judges rule their courtrooms from high in the bench. This courtroom actually felt like American justice.

From the corridor Jack peeked through the crack between the two tall doors. He didn't see attorneys' backs, or hear voices, so he assumed the Court was quiet. He walked in to find Judge Ambrose relaxing in the Jury Box, talking with his deputy bailiff and clerk. Judge Ambrose wore a white shirt and tie, sans jacket or robe.

"Hi Jack," Judge Ambrose said, grinning across his courtroom. He put his hand to his forehead as if to concentrate. "Let me guess... the Russell murder."

"As usual, Judge, you're absolutely right." Jack hadn't calmed down from the news report.

"Then we better go into my office." Judge Ambrose pushed open the jury box gate and stepped out. He shook Jack's hand. "How are Sarah and the kids?"

"Good, Judge. Everyone's good."

"Excellent. Tell her I said hello." The Judge walked around the front of the bench to a door leading into a corridor. This corridor connected to every courtroom on the floor, and had a private elevator for the judges. The Judge's chamber was directly behind his courtroom.

Jack took a seat in front of the red cherry desk with Judge Ambrose behind. The Judge eyed him. "You've got quite a case, Jack."

"It's breaking open, Judge, but there are twists."

"I thought as much. What do you need?"

Jack told Judge Ambrose the details, and before he finished, Judge Ambrose nodded, already knowing what Jack needed. When Jack paused, Judge Ambrose said: "I'll write the order to get Kyle to California."

"Thanks Judge," Jack said.

Within a few minutes the Judge had drafted and signed the order. "Good luck, my friend. Be careful. Your family needs you around."

Jack ran the order down to the Superior Court Clerk and had it imprinted, then he hurried it back to the office. Here was the key to Angola State Penitentiary and the secrets of Kyle Sanders.

TWENTY-ONE

Danny smiled when he saw the freeway sign for the airport. He desperately needed two things, and both would be there.

He pulled into a seedy neighborhood full of rundown government housing: two-story red-brick apartments landscaped with cement and half-dead crabgrass. Near every third building a broken-down swing set sat in a bedding of dried-up tan bark. Cyclone fencing lined the perimeter. Curtains wafted outside screen-less open windows. The front doors on some the apartments hung open. Children in diapers played in the dirt, their hands and faces filthy. No one watched them.

Lucky I'm not a child molester, Danny thought. *I could take any one of them.*

The ground shook as jets thundered overhead. The children seemed unaware that they were growing up on the end of a runway.

Danny spotted the dope dealer. Dope dealers looked the same in every ghetto, there, on the corner with no intention to cross. They watched everything, heads swiveling constantly. The slightest hint of a cop would send them running on a pre-determined route, usually over fences.

Danny rolled up in his car and waived the dealer to his window. The guy looked around, then approached. It took Danny exactly twenty seconds to score his beloved crank. *Why can't supermarkets be so efficient?*

From the ghetto Danny headed straight for the airport, then followed the signs to the long-term parking lot. Danny grabbed a ticket from the machine. The arm lifted and folded away so he could drive in. He parked in an area crowded with cars and close to the pick-up area for the shuttle bus.

His luck with the cold plate at the last motel sucked. He wasn't going to make the same mistake twice. He needed to dump this car for one that would stay cold for at least a couple of days. Danny tried his shaved key in two cars without luck. The third was a charm.

When Danny drove back out the parking attendant looked at him and his ticket. "You've only been here eight minutes."

"I took a wrong turn, then I got confused. Took me awhile to find my way out."

The attendant gave Danny a look of disgust. The gate lifted. The attendant waived Danny through without taking any money.

Danny headed straight for his sister's with his crank and his very cold car.

* * *

When Jack returned from court he was thankful he could slip through the side door. The media had taken over the front lobby. Extended booms with satellite dishes reached into the sky. Both street and parking lot were lined with coaches from every major station. Jack was surprised no one was selling silk-screened T-Shirts adorned with Lisa's face. The crime scene and the leak had put the story back in the lead. They were starved for details, but Jack wasn't about to give them any. They were close to putting this one down.

When Jack got back in the office things were moving. Casey had the Ramey Warrant for Danny, and Andrew was looking for Jack.

"Jack, Herman Porter emailed me the six-pack," Andrew said. "I printed it and gave it to Richards."

"Excellent, Cody Sines will tighten things up when he picks out Danny."

Jack and Casey met with Richards, and saw the image of Danny. This one's eyes looked steely cold.

"He cut his hair. It's shorter than what the bartender described," said Richards.

"Good… sign of guilt. He's trying to change his appearance."

"Do you want to show the six-pack to the bartender, or do you want someone else to go?" Richards asked.

"I'd rather you send someone else. Casey and I need to get moving."

"Got it," Richards left to find another detective and returned quickly. "It's on its way."

"Thanks, Boss. Casey and I need to brief the Mayor and his wife. We'll let them know we have a suspect and we're trying to locate him."

"I'm surprised it hasn't been leaked yet," said Richards.

"After we brief the Mayor, we'll head straight to Texas. Hopefully, we can get Fields wrapped up, then hop over to Angola and grab Kyle."

Richards nodded. "I'll handle the media. I'll confirm Lisa was murdered in the park. I haven't figured out yet what the hell to say about Kyle."

"Just try to keep them about two steps behind us." *Such a crazy relationship,* Jack thought. *We chase the bad guys and the media chase us. And we always have to keep that gap between us and them until the end.*

* * *

This time Jack was glad to meet with the Mayor. Now they were on the road to doing something good, the first step in healing the loss. Without answers closure never occurs.

They sat in the same living room, this time with Mrs. Russell there. Jack was glad to see she was able to get out of bed. Collectively, the four of them looked like they had been to Hell and back. The Mayor's own spirit and life had drained out of him. Mrs. Russell's eyes moved but never focused, a symptom of heavy sedation.

"Sir, we've identified a suspect," Jack let the news sink in.

"Is he in custody? Has he confessed?" The Mayor's hands started to shake. Jack didn't know if it was from shock or anger.

"He's not in custody, sir. We believe he's in Texas. We're heading there now to find him."

"I see... We... my wife and I saw the news report. Who is this man in prison that knew about Lisa?"

"It's someone that sent us details about the case. Casey and I met him. He wants to be moved in exchange for information." Jack realized his answer sounded confusing without the background information.

"There was an eye witness to the murder?" The Mayor looked shocked.

"Not that kind of witness, sir. This man has been locked up in Angola State Penitentiary for sixteen years. He committed a murder when he was young and was sentenced to life in prison."

"I'm sorry, but I'm a little confused, Jack. You already know who killed Lisa, right?"

"Yes, Sir. I believe we do. But, this guy knows details about the murder. He told us details before we even identified the suspect." Jack went slowly. "We have to find out how he knew. We cannot leave it open. The bottom line, Sir, we negotiated a deal with him. We're bringing him back to California to do his time, and then he'll talk to us."

"You can do that?"

Jack nodded.

"Can you tell us his name? The name of the man that killed Lisa?" It was the first words Mrs. Russell spoke.

Jack looked at her and saw her eyes were focused on his. "Danny Fields. We believe Danny killed Lisa."

"I never heard of him. Did Lisa know him?" Mrs. Russell asked.

"We don't think so, but we're not sure yet."

Jack did not disclose that the case did not appear random. He didn't have answers for the questions they would ask. Instead he gave an abridged version.

He saw the pain and disgust in their faces as he

reached the part about the Trooper Haynes. They saw that others were losing so much to Danny Fields. As he finished all four of them stared at one another, each caught up in thoughts, processing information, and wondering.

"Sir, the media is all over the case and as usual, we wanted you to hear the facts from us rather than from a leak," Casey said.

"Thank you both very much for your hard work gentlemen. We appreciate it very much." The Mayor stood up. "You're obviously quite busy. We don't want to stand in your way."

"Sir, we appreciate your confidence. We'll keep you posted."

Jack and Casey left the Mayor and his wife standing in the doorway with their arms around one another.

* * *

When Jack and Casey returned Andrew was waiting.

"Big news guys! The lab called, Lisa came back positive with Rohypnol. You were right Jack, she was drugged."

"It's coming together," Jack said. "There's something else, right?"

"There sure is, the gun matches! The same gun killed Lisa and Trooper Haynes," Andrew paused a second then dropped the bomb. "Cody Sines picked out Danny in the six-pack. It's a positive identification Jack. You guys got him!"

I knew it would all match up, Jack thought. It felt good to finally hear the words.

Jack looked at Casey. "You ready to go get Danny?"

"Ready as I'll ever be."

"Then let's go."

190

TWENTY-TWO

Jack and Casey landed in Texas and rented a non-descript SUV. Jack drove and Casey navigated.

"Let's go see Herman Porter," said Jack.

"We didn't call ahead. You think he'll be there?"

"From the sound of Herman, he'll be there."

"Why didn't we call ahead?"

"I'm not real trusting of cops I don't know. I feel better if they don't know when we're coming."

Casey changed the subject. "This is a nice SUV," He rubbed the sill under the window.

"Yeah, we can disable the automatic headlights at night, and become stealth. Plus, we'll be in it day and night. We don't have a hotel reservation.

"Did the Nevada Troopers say when they were coming down?"

"Late tonight. I plan on us being on Danny before they touch down."

Casey gave Jack directions to the Texas State Trooper Headquarters. On this, his second trip south within forty-eight hours, Jack felt hot and tired. He was relieved when the building's air conditioning hit him full blast. The officer behind the counter reminded Jack of the prison officer at Angola.

"Hello, gentlemen. How can I help you?" He was as polite as a concierge in a 5-star hotel.

Is everyone down here this polite? Jack wondered. *Where are the pissed-off front desk cops I'm used to?*

"Hello officer, we're from the San Francisco Police Department-Homicide. I've been speaking with Detective Herman Porter from your agency." Jack held out his credentials.

"Yes, Sir, Detective Porter is here, but he didn't say he was expecting ya'll." The officer inspected Jack's badge and identification card.

"Sorry. That's not his fault. We've been working on this case and weren't sure when we would get here." Jack said.

"He did tell me there were some fellas coming from Nevada. I believe they'll be here later tonight."

Jack smiled. *I guess Nevada cops are a lot more trusting than I am.*

"Let me call Detective Porter for ya'll," The officer picked up the phone and had a short conversation. Jack couldn't hear what he whispered into the phone. Within seconds, a handsome gentleman came in from a secured door.

Detective Porter was a slight man with perfectly groomed hair and a well-tailored, lightweight navy blue suit. His yellow tie had touches of violet that accented the subtle stripe in his suit. His white shirt had medium starch with a French cuff. His cufflinks matched the violet, and his Italian shoes had stylish buckles on the side. Herman wore a small pin in his left lapel indicating he was a detective. He was exactly what Jack imagined from the phone call: he looked like a Southern Baptist television preacher.

Detective Porter extended his soft hand. "Hello gentlemen, I'm Herman Porter." No titles or rank.

"Hello Herman, I'm Jack. This is Casey Ford."

"I didn't expect ya'll so soon. I thought you might call first." Porter raised an eyebrow.

"Herman, I apologize for not calling ahead. As you know, we're looking for Danny Fields," Jack said. Porter clearly knew they'd never intended to call ahead.

"I understand."

"By the way, thank you for the six-pack you sent us. We got a positive identification on Danny with it."

"Excellent! I have some other information for you as well. Come with me, please." Porter unlocked the secured door and held it open for Jack and Casey. They walked down a short hallway into a small detective office. There was nobody else there.

"I understand you are conducting a joint investigation with the Nevada State Police?"

"Yes, we are." Jack stumbled on his answer. "You see, we're working together to some degree, but in reality, we're not."

"Okay, I see."

"Frankly, we are truly sorry for the Trooper and his family. Personally, I hope he gets executed behind it. But, the Mayor's daughter is our priority."

"I understand completely."

"Thank you," said Jack.

"Gentlemen, as I have explained. We cannot assist you to a level you might expect from a large department. We're short-staffed and overworked. I'm sorry I can't provide you with sworn personnel to travel to the areas where ya'll are going."

"Where are we going?" asked Jack.

"Here are four addresses Danny used while in Texas. He did time in Texas for sexual battery. It was originally a rape charge, but it got reduced. He did an eight-year stint in Louisiana for forcible rape. He got out three months ago and absconded parole."

"Where in Louisiana did he did he do his time?" Jack chewed his lip waiting for the answer.

"Angola, why?"

"We have a snitch in Angola that said the killer told him he was planning to murder our victim."

"Interesting, what's his name?"

"Kyle Sanders. He's been in sixteen years for murder."

"Have you checked him in the Family Court files?"

"No, I don't think we can do that from California." Jack had never heard of a Family Court File.

"We have good reciprocal files with Louisiana. That's how I got the address for Danny's sister's house." Herman pointed to a paper on the table that was highlighted. "I ran a credit check on him. He once listed her on a credit card application as a referral. I ran a check on her and she still owns the same house as she did back then. She's never been arrested and has a good driving record. There is also a printout of a vehicle that is registered to her. She has never received welfare and has never been lawfully married." Porter smiled.

"Outstanding work, Herman." Jack said, genuinely impressed.

"Give me the details on Kyle Sanders. I'll see what I can do."

Jack gave Herman Kyle's vitals.

"I gave you the other addresses just to be thorough. I think they're crash pads at best, but they're all pretty close to his sister's house. You gentlemen have a three-hour drive ahead. Can I get you something to eat before you take off?"

"No thank you, Herman. We're anxious to get going."

"I listed the numbers for the local Sheriff, the Parish Police and the State Police on back of one of those pages. You may need them."

"Herman, you've been a great help. Thank you."

"My pleasure gentlemen, I wish I could join you. There is nothing more I would rather do than nail Danny."

They exchanged business cards and cell phone numbers. Herman gave them written directions to the county where Danny's sister lived. They were back on the highway. The cool air from the air conditioner felt good on Jack's face.

"I like the way he works," said Jack.

"Me too," said Casey. The younger cop shielded the nervousness in his voice.

* * *

Danny had relaxed for a couple of days. His sister's house hadn't changed since his last visit. He hadn't seen her since he arrived so he figured she was out of town for a while. No big deal. She always loved when he popped in for a visit. She was a creature of habit. She always left a spare key in a small wooden shoe in the outside laundry room. Danny found the key and helped himself to her food, full bar, clean shower and linens.

Her ranch style house was modest, in a neighborhood surrounded by similar homes. They were small, but comfortable, and cleverly situated on small lots to afford the most privacy. It was a perfect place to hide out for a couple of months.

Even if the neighbors noticed him, it didn't matter; he belonged. This was his sister's house. She welcomed him, even though she wasn't home.

As he parked his newly-acquired vehicle in the driveway, Danny felt safe.

TWENTY-THREE

By the time Jack and Casey found Danny's sister's house it was the middle of the night. There was no light but that from the street.

"There's a car in the driveway. Can you catch the plate, Casey?" Jack shut off their headlights as they came up on the address.

"Yeah, got it! It's not the same one Porter gave us."

"I don't see the car Porter gave us anywhere," said Jack.

"Me neither. I'll call our communications and run this plate." Casey dialed his cell phone, gave details and hung up.

Jack parked three houses away on the opposite side of the street. They had a good view of the front of the house and the car.

Casey's cell phone buzzed. He answered it, and Jack listened, keeping his eyes on the house.

"Okay...it isn't hot? Do us a favor, call the registered owner and see if they know where their car is. Sure, I'll hang on." Casey glanced at Jack. Jack nodded in agreement. "Yeah, I'm still here," Casey said. He listened for a moment. "No, that's all for now. Just leave a message on their answering machine. Hopefully they'll call back." Casey hung up.

"The R/O lives three hours from here."

"It's hot. Danny stole it, and he's in there," said Jack.

They sat in silence for several minutes. Jack felt edgy. "Danny is extremely dangerous and we're on our own. We need to keep our cool, okay?"

"I hear you, Jack."

"Let's hop in the back seat. The windows are tinted darker and we won't get spotted." The two men climbed over the console between the front seats, nearly kicking each other in the process. Once back there they settled in. Casey munched on sunflower seeds. They had several bottles of water. It was just enough for a long night.

A few hours later dawn light shone in the east.

"Stake-outs were easier when I was younger," Jack yawned. He stretched and twisted at the waist. In the cramped space it was the best he could do.

"I could sure use a cup of coffee." Casey's voice grated from lack of sleep and too many sunflower seeds.

"I agree. Hey, Casey, hand me the bottle."

Casey passed the empty plastic water bottle to Jack. Jack cut the top off so he could pee in it.

"One time I was on this stake-out all night."

"Yeah?"

"I had to piss so bad I couldn't think straight. I split to a gas station for two minutes. When I got back, the guy was gone."

"That sucks."

"From then on...I piss in a bottle," said Jack as he filled the bottle.

"Jack! There's our guy! He just came out of the house. He's putting a jacket or something in the car." Casey pointed.

Jack didn't dare look up until he was finished.

Casey gave a play-by-play. "Yep, that's definitely him. He's squirrelly, checking everything out. Hey, he's looking our way! Duck!" Casey slid lower into the rear seat. Jack tried to do the same, but his situation was a bit more complicated.

"What's he doing now?" Jack finished his business without spilling.

"He's going back inside. He may be getting ready to leave." Casey sat up straight.

Jack got an adrenaline rush that made him forget his sore body. "Did he spot us?"

"He eye-balled our car, but there's no way he could have seen us back here."

* * *

Danny went out to throw a light jacket in the car. He figured he'd gotten his use out from the car, and planned to drive it a few miles away and dump it. Then he spotted the SUV a few houses away. *Was that there last night?* he wondered. He couldn't remember. But unexplained SUVs and vans made him nervous. Some might call it paranoia, but Danny knew it was just being safe. He decided to stay put. *You die if you fly,* he thought. This bird would avoid the hunter.

Danny tucked his 9mm pistol in the front of his pants, then went out the back door and walked around the house towards the front fence. He grabbed a wooden crate and placed it next to the fence so he could peek over. He watched the SUV.

* * *

Jack quickly ran through their limited choices. "Option one: we let him split and try tailing him while we call in for help from the locals. Problem is it's daylight and we only got one car. We'd get burned in a heartbeat."

"I agree," said Casey.

"Option two: let him get in the car, then jam him. But I don't think this SUV will block the entire driveway. It's too wide."

"Plus, we don't have car-stop capabilities," said Casey. "No red light or siren. If he runs we're screwed."

"Option three: call and wait for back-up. If Danny splits, we explain to Richards and the Mayor why we let him drive away." Jack winced at the thought.

"Option four: I hit the front and you go to the rear."

"Okay," said Casey.

Jack grabbed the door handle, and held that position. His breath was heavy from excitement. Casey held the same position at the other door.

"Nice and slow, buddy," Jack said. "Let's go get that asshole! Ready?"

"Ready."
They opened their doors and got out.

* * *

Danny saw the rear passenger doors of the SUV open. Two guys in suits got out. They moved quickly towards the house. Danny felt the bottom fall out of his stomach. A wind gust blew one guy's jacket open. Danny saw the glint of a badge, a glimpse of a gun. *Shit! How did they find me here?*

He considered shooting them, then realized they may not be alone. He should have looked around for other vehicles or cops. He'd had tunnel-vision for the SUV. Now he scanned the street. No other cops in view, and he hadn't seen any climbing over the back fence.

If he fired now, everyone would hear the gunshots, and the place would be crawling with cops within minutes. *They must've spotted me when I went to the car. Why hide? They know I'm here.*

Danny had his own options, but all of them sucked. He saw the bigger cop head towards the front door. He lost sight of the second cop but he figured that one was coming around back. Danny quickly retreated towards the outside laundry room and hid in the heavy cover of the bushes. Within seconds, the smaller cop appeared near the corner of the house. He was crouched low and moved slowly. His gun was drawn, pointing forward.

Did he see me hide? Danny's heart pounded so hard he thought the cop could hear it. The cop paused and scanned the yard. He looked back and forth between the back of the house and the laundry room. The cop was in a tactical dilemma and Danny knew it. He didn't feel safe with his back to the laundry room without first checking to see if it was clear.

The cop moved slowly across the lawn. He stared directly at Danny while he advanced. Danny couldn't believe the cop couldn't see him. Danny's hands shook so badly it was hard to steady his gun. Sweat poured down his face, stinging his eyes. He aimed through the bushes, squeezed one eye shut and put the bead of his gun sight directly on the cop's forehead. He put pressure on the trigger and felt the hammer draw back.

The cop was ten feet away and closing the distance quickly. Danny was a split second from blowing his head off when he realized the cop wasn't looking at him. He was moving towards the laundry room doorway. The cop hadn't spotted him. Danny eased the pressure on the trigger. The cop passed within three feet of him, then disappeared into the laundry room.

Perfect! Danny heard the faint sound of wood breaking inside. A voice—the other cop—yelled: "Police!" Danny knew the other cop would be busy searching the house for a few minutes. Danny followed behind the cop who'd entered the laundry room. He had the washer and dryer to his left and a small folding table to his right. The cop was opening a vented closet door at the rear with one hand while pointing his gun with the other.

Danny put his gun to the back of the cop's head and said with eerie calmness: "Freeze or I'll blow your fucking brains out."

The cop did it, tensing up like a tiger.

"Have you ever wondered if you hear the gunshot when you get shot in the head at point-blank range?"

"No."

"You don't want to find out. So, nice and slow, slide your gun across the floor."

The cop hesitated.

"Hey, asshole, you're taking too long!"

The cop put his gun on the floor and slid it away.

"Get on your knees and put your arms straight out."

The cop complied. Danny searched around the cop's waistband while holding the gun to his head. He took the handcuffs that hung from the rear of the waistband.

"Do you carry a backup? Don't lie, or you'll die."

"I don't carry a backup. You got my only gun."

"Put your hands behind your back."

The cop complied.

Danny squeezed the handcuffs on him as tight as he could. Asshole cops had done it to him enough times. It felt good to give it back. Danny liked controlling this cop. It felt almost as good as raping a bitch that deserved it.

Danny rolled the cop on his side and searched the rest of his body for a gun. Luckily for the cop, Danny didn't find a backup. He grabbed the cop's gun off the floor, made sure the hammer wasn't cocked, then slipped the gun in his back waistband. Danny reached over, grabbed the cop's sleeve and said: "Get up!"

Danny tucked himself in as tight as he could behind the cop. He grabbed the back of the man's hair with one hand, stuck his gun to the side of his head and asked, "What's your partner's name?"

"Jack."

"Let's go talk to Jack. Nice and slow, asshole. Keep your mouth shut or I'll kill you. Got it?"

The cop nodded.

They walked slowly across the backyard towards the rear door. Danny opened it and they stepped into the all white kitchen. Danny heard Jack searching another part of the house.

"Shhhhh... don't say a word," he whispered. They stood motionless in the middle of the kitchen. Danny kept the muzzle of his gun pressed into the side of the cop's head. Minutes felt like hours. Danny heard Jack moving closer towards the kitchen. Danny decided not to call out. That would give Jack the tactical advantage. Danny wanted Jack to be surprised. He planned to take off Jack the same way, then leave them handcuffed together so he could split. Killing these cops wouldn't make his escape any easier.

Jack turned the corner into the kitchen and froze. After a split second he raised his gun, then began backing out of the kitchen.

"Not so fast, Jack! If you back out of here, I'm

gonna kill your partner."

Jack stopped, but kept his gun pointed at them.

"Jack, put your gun on the floor and slide it towards me, nice and easy."

"Go fuck yourself!" said Jack.

Danny was well concealed behind the cop. Jack didn't have a shot.

"Casey, you okay?" asked Jack.

"Hey Jack, I'm running this show, not you! Shut up!" said Danny.

Casey yelled, "Don't do it Jack! He's got me handcuffed! Kill this asshole after he shoots me, or shoot us both!"

"Why'd you do it Danny? Why Lisa?" Jack knew he had to distract Danny if he were to have a shot at winning.

"Shut up and put your gun down!"

"You had it all planned out since Angola. Kyle Sanders told us."

"Who? What?"

"Kyle Sanders...Angola...You know?"

"I don't know what the fuck you're talking about! Shut your mouth, now!"

"Did you do it alone, Danny? Or did you have a friend help you?"

"You don't know what you're talking about. That stuck-up bitch got what she deserved. She thought she could treat me like garbage!"

Jack kept his aim. He could only see a small portion of Danny's head.

"Jack, I'm telling you!" Danny screamed. "Don't be stupid. I'm gonna cuff you up like your friend and I'll be on my way."

Casey screamed, "Jack, don't do it. He's lying. Shoot Jack! I forgive you, I promise! Shoot us both! Don't let him walk out of here!"

"Jack, don't listen to your partner. I could have already killed him and you. I have no need to kill you too. Don't make me do it. Put your gun on the floor."

"Kyle Sanders, you remember him, right? Angola?"

Jack tried to keep Danny talking.

Casey screamed hysterically, "Jesus Christ, Jack! Shoot him now!"

"Shut up asshole!" Danny screamed.

The situation was surreal. Things moved in slow motion. The screams muffled in Jack's ears, and his whole focus was his front sight and Casey's face. He could see the machined marks on the front sight of his gun. He saw red veins in Casey's eyes. Their cops' eyes locked onto one another. Jack felt like Casey was trying to tell him something.

"Jack, put down your gun. Don't be stupid, man!" yelled Danny.

"My heart, I have a bad heart!" Casey coughed and spit.

Jack kept his gun pointed at Casey's head. They were eight feet apart from one another. *Does Casey really have a bad heart? Is he setting up something?*

Jack took deep breaths, calming himself. His arms and shoulders burned as he steadied his gun.

Casey coughed harder then suddenly jerked and twisted his head sideways.

Jack saw three quarters of Danny's face. Instinctively, he squeezed the trigger. His gun exploded. The muzzle flash blinded him. He felt the fear of God. Casey and Danny fell to the floor. Jack didn't know which one he shot.

The kitchen filled with the sweet aroma of blood and burnt gunpowder. Casey rolled over onto his stomach and moaned. The side of his head and face were covered in blood. Jack saw Danny on his back on the white kitchen tile. His right eye and the top right portion of his head were blown off. His left eye was fixed open and glazed like a dead fish. His mouth was stuck open in a silent scream. Casey was covered with Danny's blood.

"Jack, get these fucking cuffs off me."

It was over. The chase ended with Danny dead on his back, in his sister's beautiful kitchen. *She'll love the police for this*, Jack thought.

***

Jack and Casey sat at the kitchen table with Danny dead on the floor. Casey's gun was still in Danny's waistband. They would wait for the local police to remove it. Jack watched Casey fumble with the cell phone. His hands shook and he had trouble dialing the local police.

Jack was already on his phone with Richards. "Hey, Boss."

"You guys got him?" Richards asked.

"Yeah...Kind of, I guess."

"Ahh shit, don't tell me?"

"Yeah, he's dead."

"Are you guys okay?"

"Yeah, we're good," Jack gave him details of the shooting.

"He didn't know Kyle?" Richards asked.

"He didn't seem to. Maybe he was lying."

"This place is a media circus. The Warden at Angola called me. He said reporters are showing up at the prison requesting an interview with Kyle for Christ's sakes! Kyle Sanders has become a household name!"

"That's insane," said Jack. Everything had become insane to him. How the hell did Kyle know about the case? How did that bitch Traci Townsend know out about Kyle? It didn't click together. One thing for sure, he was going to find out soon.

"Are you guys okay to pick up Kyle? I can send someone else."

"No, we got it. I'll keep you posted." Jack hung up.

Casey was off the phone too. "I'm so sorry, Jack. I put you in a horrible situation."

"It wasn't your fault Casey. If I went around back instead, it would have been me, not you." Jack paused a moment. "I wouldn't have been smart enough to pretend I was having a heart problem."

"Pretend? Who the hell was pretending? I thought I was going to die!"

Jack pondered a moment then said, "I don't get it, Casey. Do you think Danny was lying about Kyle?"

"I don't know, Jack. He must have been, right?"

Jack heard sirens approaching. Within seconds he heard a voice at the front door, "Police! Are you detectives in there?"

"Yeah, we're in the kitchen," Jack yelled.

TWENTY-FOUR

Kyle couldn't help but smirk as he packed his letters and hand-drawn pornographic pictures into a box. He didn't expect the detectives to move so quickly. *He wasn't complaining about it either.* The Warden himself called Kyle to his office to tell him he was being moved immediately. Kyle took great satisfaction in knowing that Justin would come to work later, and find him gone. Justin could go fuck himself, tonight, and every night from now on.

Kyle finished packing, picked up his box of worldly possessions, and called to the guard. "I'm done in here, sir!" With a loud crack the steel door electronically disengaged and fell ajar. Kyle pushed it open with his foot and stepped out onto the elevated steel walkway. He'd spent sixteen years in that tiny cell, just about every day of his adult life. All those days had been supervised and planned by other people. It never changed.

"Hey Sanders! Where you going?" an inmate yelled.

"Hey movie star! Don't tell us you're moving to Hollywood!" another screamed. Others laughed and whistled.

Kyle ignored them. He hadn't thought it would happen this fast, or ever for that matter, but finally the promise had been kept.

The guard marched him into the receiving area, usually reserved for new inmates.

"Sanders...get in the shower," he barked.

Kyle undressed and complied.

"Wash your hair and brush your teeth. I don't want you stinkin' on the flight to California."

Kyle followed directions without saying a word.

After the shower, they strip-searched him and gave him deodorant. They sat at a table on the opposite side of the metal detector, and X-rayed everything. Another guard packed his stuff into a small brown suitcase, then waved Kyle through the metal detector. Once he got to the other side, he was given underwear, socks, a pair of blue jeans, a white cotton button-up shirt and a pair of black shoes with laces removed. Laces could be used to strangle someone, or to hang himself.

Not in sixteen years had Kyle done anything like this. Breaking his daily routine seemed foreign. He would soon exit the front gate of Angola State Penitentiary long before he was dead. That wasn't supposed to happen.

Jack and Casey sat in the receiving area, their rental car was parked in the high-security lot. As the prisoner walked up carrying his suitcase Jack thought he almost looked human. Three guards escorted Kyle. Jack immediately noticed the prison shuffle, slow, with steps never more than twelve inches. That was years of muscle memory at work. Those feet would always feel shackled. Kyle stopped a few feet from Jack and Casey. He didn't speak.

"Hi Kyle, you remember us?" asked Jack.

Kyle stared.

"We're taking you to California. We got a lot to talk about, pal."

Kyle looked at both men and nodded his head. His face was expressionless.

"Put your hands out in front of you." Jack reached into his rear waistband and grabbed a pair of handcuffs from under his suit jacket.

Kyle set his suitcase at his side and complied.

"I'm going to handcuff you in the front. It's a long way back and you'll be more comfortable that way," Jack placed the cuffs on Kyle's wrist. "I'm double locking them so they won't get overly tight on you, okay?"

Kyle nodded without speaking.

Casey grabbed the small suitcase and threw it in the trunk of the rental car.

Jack opened the right front passenger door. He stepped back and told Kyle, "Get in and buckle the seat belt."

Kyle sat in the seat. He reached up with his cuffed hands to grab the seat belt. It was the first time he ever used one. They'd never had a car when he was a kid, and back then if you did get in a car no buzzers went off, making you comply. As an adult he'd only seen seatbelts on television. Casey and Jack shook hands with the guards and got in the car. Casey drove and Jack sat directly behind Kyle.

There was a loud buzzer and a bell rang out. It sounded like a fire alarm, startling Kyle. Yellow warning lights on poles came to life, spinning and throwing light like a summer lightning storm. The large steel door rolled up slowly. Kyle stared out at the world. It revealed itself little by little as the door rolled towards the ceiling. Once the door was completely opened, the alarms and flashing lights stopped. Silence fell. Casey drove through a section Kyle had never seen. Here inmates walked around unescorted, none shackled, some even holding rakes and brooms. They were working. Out here they had landscaping, bushes, trees and sidewalks. These were the low risk minimum security inmates. Kyle had known they existed, he just didn't know where. They passed through one additional security gate—the gate to the real outside world. The trees and bushes around the prison were bigger, more mature. Kyle had seen them once, sixteen years before on his way in, a lifetime ago. He remembered them like it was yesterday.

Kyle seemed mesmerized by sights and scents. As soon as they left the receiving area, he was overcome with the clean sweet odor of fresh air. He could actually smell the fresh cut lawn and flowers. For years, the only scent he experienced was the pungent odor of the cleaning disinfectant used on the floors and walls. He quickly became accustomed to the smell of men who exercised but didn't shower. He actually had forgotten how sweet the outside world smelled. This was the outside.

A voice brought him back. "Kyle, I'm going to make something very clear to you right up front." Jack leaned over the seat onto Kyle's left shoulder.

"Yes, sir," Kyle whispered softly.

"I like you, but if you so much as think to reach for that door handle, I will blow your fucking head off."

Kyle didn't take the comment as threat. He knew Jack was simply explaining the absolute truth.

"I understand, sir."

"You are a convicted murderer. I haven't a single qualm in me. Handcuffed or not, I guarantee you, I'll shoot you before I allow you to escape."

Kyle nodded and watched Casey from the corner of his eye. Casey stared straight ahead, driving.

Jack continued. "I will not be on the national news because I let you escape. Quite frankly, nobody would give a damn if I killed you."

"Yes, sir, you're right."

"When we get to the airport, you're in custody for check fraud. We're extraditing you to California, got it?"

"Yes, sir."

"If we told them you were a murderer, the captain would never let us on the plane. We'd be driving back to California. And frankly, I'm not in the mood."

"Yes, sir."

Jack moved away from Kyle and sat back in his seat. "Oh Kyle, one more thing."

"Yes, sir?"

"Stop calling me 'sir.' I'm a detective."

"Yes...Detective."

They drove about twenty minutes without speaking.

Jack started the conversation. "Kyle, why don't you start telling us about the murder and how you know the details you had in the letter?"

Kyle felt a sense of panic. He didn't have a shred of information except what was in that letter, and Jack would quickly figure it out. He hesitated a moment and looked towards Casey to see if he was going to say something. *Now would be a good time*, he thought. Casey said nothing. He stared out the front windshield. He looked lost in thought and oblivious to Jack's question.

Kyle stalled. "I will, Detective, just like I said I would. I'd feel a lot more comfortable if I started talking once we were on that jet. It'd be a lot harder for ya'll to turn around and take me back." He hoped Jack accepted the excuse.

Jack paused a long moment. It was dead quiet in the car. "Alright Kyle, I understand how you feel. Plus, it's a long flight."

"Hey, Jack, I got to take a leak," said Casey. "You mind if we pull over?" He looked at Jack in the rear view mirror.

"Fine with me," Jack said, looking around at the empty landscape. "Stop anywhere, there's nothing out here."

"How about you?" Casey asked Kyle.

"I got to piss too, if ya'll let me."

"Alright, I'll pull over and get you out."

Kyle wasn't sure how this worked, so he just followed along.

* * *

Richards made all the necessary notifications; first, about the shooting and then that Jack and Casey were picking up Kyle. He had to get the Mayor up to speed so that there would be no embarrassing surprises. He needed to brief the Press Information Officers. He did this personally so they would understand exactly what information they could release to the media. Reporters would be all over this thing within hours.

Richards' pager kept going off but he didn't even look to see who was calling. He had enough on his plate.

When he finally checked it, he realized Andrew was trying to get through. The damn thing was an emergency page. *What now?* he thought. This happened just as Richards entered his office. Andrew was right there, with another phone message in hand.

"What's this?" Richards growled.

"Herman Porter called, said it's urgent, sir."

"Who the Hell is Herman Porter?"

"The Detective in Texas who helped Jack and Casey. He sent that six-pack too."

"That's right. Jesus Christ! Does everybody have an emergency?"

Richards went into his office, closed the door and dialed the number.

"This is Porter!" The Texan's voice was hurried.

"Porter, this is Lieutenant Richards. You called?"

"I think Jack's in trouble, Lieutenant!"

"What? Have you talked to him? Is he okay?"

"I tried him, but his cell phone doesn't work out there at the prison."

"I'm not following, Porter...If you haven't talked to him, how do you..."

"Lieutenant, please! Casey Ford and Kyle Sanders are half-brothers!"

"What? How do you know?"

"It's a long story, sir. But when Jack mentioned Sanders I said I would check some reciprocal systems between Texas and Louisiana, beyond criminal history stuff, okay? I looked at family-and-welfare. Kyle has a half-brother, and his name is Casey Ford!"

"What the hell!"

"That's what I thought too. It couldn't be, right? But it is—same mother, different fathers. When they were kids she got welfare on both!"

"My God! And they're out there—"

"I tried to call Jack but the area around the prison has no cell service," Porter rasped.

"It's a setup," Richards cried.

"Looks like it," Porter said.

"Lemme call Angola and see if they're there yet." Richards felt like he was going to vomit.

"Okay...I'll..."

Richards hung up, just as he noticed a number scrawled on a notepad. Jack had written it. It was for Angola. Richards punched the keys. He tried to tell the prison operator it was life-and-death, but he was suddenly on hold, then a mechanical voice transferred him around. A minute passed like an hour, then finally an officer identified himself—a real human being.

"This is Lieutenant Richards, San Francisco PD. Are the detectives still there?"

"No sir, they left with the inmate about thirty minutes ago. Is there a problem, sir?"

"I just learned that Casey Ford, our new homicide man who's with Jack Paige, is Sanders's half-brother. It all stinks of setup—a breakout, and Jack's gonna be the victim."

"Holy Shit!" said the guard. "We'll dispatch a team of guards immediately. There's only one road in and out, sir!"

Richards hung up without taking the phone from his ear. He called the operator and got the Baton Rouge Airport Police. Next, he ran to the Chief's office. The whole way he wondered if Jack was still alive.

* * *

Casey pulled the car to a stop onto the soft dirt shoulder. There was little room to park because the road was elevated about four feet from the surrounding flat terrain. Jack had noticed roadways built the same way in places where rainfall was high. It kept the road from flooding.

For miles there was nothing but bushes, sparse trees and mosquitoes. Jack didn't have to pee, so he wouldn't venture far from the car.

Casey shut off the engine, left the keys in the ignition, and he and Jack got out. Jack stretched, gulping hot humid air. His head was still foggy from the shooting. This marsh felt peaceful, like it hadn't changed in a million years. Cricket chirps mixed into a continuous insect buzz, like a natural mantra.

"I'm going to take a leak, then I'll take care of Kyle," Casey edged down the embankment, balancing himself with outspread arms. Jack watched Casey disappear behind some bushes fifty yards away. The older detective glanced up and down the desolate road. It was incredibly peaceful. Footsteps made him jump. It was Casey climbing the embankment towards the car. Jack marveled at how the lush landscape soaked up sounds of movement.

"Get out," Casey said to the prisoner as he opened the door.

Kyle unbuckled his seat belt and turned his body so his feet were out the door and on the ground. He had to rock his body forward a bit so he could get out without the use of his handcuffed hands.

"We'll be right back, Jack," Casey grabbed Kyle's arm to help him down the embankment.

The two walked side-by-side.

Once they'd gone a few yards Kyle whispered, "What's next?"

"Shhh, not now," Casey hissed without so much as a glance at Kyle.

Jack watched Casey and Kyle head towards the same bushes Casey had used a moment before. Something seemed off, but he didn't know what. *Maybe just being out here with this guy, and after all that shit in Texas, all this peace,* Jack thought. But somehow it was more than that. He could sense it.

He kept worrying as Casey and Kyle disappeared behind the bushes. Jack stared after them. *Am I paranoid? Did the shooting screw me up that badly?*

Once they were out of Jack's sight, Casey took out his key and removed Kyle's cuffs. "Take a piss, Kyle," he said.

Kyle undid his button and zipper and started to pee. "I can't believe you did it, you got me out," Kyle whispered. "But what are we going to do about your partner?"

"I'll take care of that. When it's time, you run like hell and don't stop. Jack's too far away. He'll never be able to hit you."

"Okay, then what?" Kyle's hands quivered as he zipped himself up.

"Here's three thousand in cash. That should hold

you for a couple of months. Call me in a couple of weeks so I know you're safe." Casey took a sealed envelope from his inside jacket pocket and handed it to Kyle.

"I love you, Casey. Thanks for not forgetting me." As Kyle took the envelope his eyes welled with tears. He hugged his brother.

There was a sudden rustling, and the two men looked up to see Jack. He stared at them. "Something looked wrong." He'd begun figuring what was wrong with the picture even before he started across the marsh. They'd walked this way with Casey out ahead—it was backwards.

As Jack had gotten down in the brush he'd realized his partner wasn't even paying any attention to the prisoner's movements... not even a hand on Kyle to control him.

Christ, he thought, *they might as well be a couple of guys out for a walk in the woods. The cop walks behind. The cop controls. It's natural.*

But as Jack came within sight of them, and saw these two hugging, he realized everything was wrong.

"J-Jack," Casey stammered. "You don't understand. It wasn't supposed to go this way."

"I'm not following... What the hell are you talking about? What's going on?" Jack asked. He wished he'd drawn his gun.

Kyle stepped sideways, then stopped. He eyed them both.

"Kyle needs to escape, Jack. It's all going to be on me, my fault. You have nothing to do with it."

"Casey, I don't understand what you're involved in, but nothing has happened that can't be fixed."

"No..." Casey struggled for words.

"It can," Jack said, astonished at the calmness in his voice. He didn't feel calm at all.

"No Jack, you're wrong! Jack, Kyle's my half-brother. They locked him up for an accident! He was just a kid! You don't understand! He raised me! He took care of me!"

Jack's jaw dropped. He knew one thing: this was deep shit!

"I promised him, Jack. I wouldn't forget him in there. I wouldn't let him rot like garbage." Casey was crying. "I promised. It wasn't fair! He didn't deserve it!"

Jack spoke more for time than anything else. "So, you fed him the details... made him the important witness... right?"

"Appeals are bullshit here! Not like California. It's not fair, Jack! You don't understand. You've never had to live in this shit!"

"And you leaked to Traci..." The pieces suddenly fit for Jack. "Telling her guaranteed the heat. We *had* to get Kyle out. You knew that would force it, whether we solved the case or not."

"Jack, please. Let him run. It's on me. I've thought about this my entire career! I know what I'm doing...Please."

"You know I can't Casey. You'll have to kill me."

Casey turned slightly, then grabbed for his gun.

Jack's world went into slow motion. *Crazy! Casey's my partner.* Jack reached for his gun, moved right, and hunched, putting Kyle between them. Casey was a half-second ahead. *Damn him!* Jack pictured his gun out, and his finger squeezing the trigger. *If my body can just catch up.*

Casey rotated right, around Kyle. Kyle hunched, and ducked his head. He saw they were using him as cover.

Jack heard rapid pops, saw fire spit from Casey's gun, and thought someone hit him in the chest with a sledgehammer. It knocked the air from his lungs. Pain burned through his chest, like being impaled on a red-hot poker. Jack landed on his back still gripping his gun. *Two guys,* he thought. *Which one's Casey?* One man dropped to the ground. The other still stood. Jack mustered all his strength, raised his gun and fired. He didn't know if his bullet hit the mark. Jack saw Sarah and the kids, then all went dark.

TWENTY-FIVE

Lieutenant Richards personally escorted Sarah and the kids on the longest flight of their lives. He shielded them from the media gauntlet in Louisiana. A sensational story had just gone nuclear: the murder of a mayor's daughter, two brothers in a prison break, a good cop gone bad—or was he bad all along? A gunfight between cops, with a vicious murderer chained in the middle—it was all wrapped in one huge story.

The good cop lived.

Not long after his family arrived they moved Jack from the Intensive Care Unit into a private room. He remembered intense pain, falling and shooting. The time between the shooting and waking up was blank. Whole days were gone. He didn't care. Jack was lucky to be alive.

The 9mm bullet had struck his chest right of center, then shattered when it hit a rib. A fragment tore through his right lung, causing it to collapse. A surgeon repaired the lung during an 8-hour operation.

It just wasn't my time to go, he thought. Had Porter not called Richards, and had Richards not called Angola, they would not have sent a rescue team. In another few minutes he would have bled to death. The guards found him, treated his sucking chest wound and minimized his massive bleeding. A medical chopper airlifted him to the trauma center. They saved his life.

Sarah sat on the bed feeding him ice chips.

"I love you," Jack said in a hoarse voice.

"I know." She smiled, and gave him another ice chip.

When Richards had run through the entire sequence of events, Jack tried to follow, but the story seemed as hazy as the morphine fog. In the end it sickened him.

His feelings about Casey were mixed. How could a cop do that? This guy had already shown himself as a good detective. But this guy was his brother, and that's a bond that's made for extreme behavior, both good and bad, since biblical times. And now both brothers were dead, Kyle from a badly aimed shot of Casey's.

Jack wished he hadn't killed Casey. He would carry that the rest of his life. He was glad it was Casey's bullet that had killed Kyle and not his. At least that had a strange justice.

Jack felt a nagging guilt for not sensing something about Casey. He didn't say it, but those closest to him knew he thought it. But no one had seen it, not in all the years Casey had been in law enforcement. No one had sensed the plan. *Plain and simple, he was dirty,* Jack thought. *Sad, but true.*

Jack was thankful he was alive.

"Jack, you did one helluva' job. The Mayor is going to give you a commendation. Every talk show and news station wants an interview," Richards told him.

Sarah rubbed Jack's leg over the covers. "I think this would be a good time to hang it up. Don't you, honey?"

Commendations and retirement were the furthest things from Jack's mind. He just wanted to get strong enough to spend a couple of weeks in some warm Miami sun. After that he could answer all these questions—from the scene of some other crime.

This book is published by The Firm in Morgan Hill, California, with assistance from Bear Press Editorial Services through www.lulu.com.
If you would like more copies of this, or any of the books below, click to www.lulu.com, and type the title into their search box.

Other recommendations include:

Touched by Fire: One Man's Journey from Alabama to Dallas, 1954 to 1963
by Frank Griffin

The Tuxedo Park Almanac
by The Almanac Project

The Greg Kihn Almanac
by The Almanac Project

Wayne Farquhar is a police lieutenant with the San Jose, California Police Department. He is a 27 year veteran and has worked as a detective in Homicide, Sexual Assaults, Child Exploitation, Vice and Internal Affairs. Wayne spent over ten years working as a Hostage Negotiator. He lives with his wife and son in the San Francisco Bay Area.